CW00486388

HUSH HUSH

ERIK CARTER

ISBN: 9798741556306

CHAPTER ONE

Titusville, Florida
The 1990s

IT WAS the perfect place to vanish.

Amber Lund's mind always turned to that dark notion when she drove this isolated four-lane highway through an endless expanse of marshland.

She could picture a Cadillac packed with mobsters exiting onto one of the few dirt paths that branched off the highway, finding a nice patch of murk, popping the trunk, and depositing a heavy, six-foot, person-shaped bundle into the inky water.

She thought of murder weapons tossed into the primordial tangle, getaway vehicles slowly descending into swamp water, bubbles tracing up the sides, popping on the surface where the roof disappeared from existence.

She imagined corpses and the alligators that would find them. Limbs torn from torsos. Flesh and muscle stripped from bones. Yellowed, reptilian teeth destroying faces and fingerprints and dental records and all other identifying, incriminating elements.

They were dark, dark thoughts, but Amber knew they were nothing but novelties, the active imagination of a person who had read a few too many thrillers and detective stories but didn't have the anger inside her to honk her horn when she was cut off in traffic. Yes, it was all those damn books she'd read throughout her life, a habit that her uncle engrained in her by reading *Nancy Drew* and *Kara, Kid Detective* books to her as a young child.

All the stories she'd devoured through the years were the reason she couldn't drive State Road 50 in Central Florida without thinking about what a perfect place it was to make things and people vanish. It was an east-west thoroughfare bisecting the state into northern and southern halves, and the section between Orlando and the Atlantic Coast at Titusville was filled with miles of barely touched nature, a flat horizon of grassy marshland stretching in all directions, a plane of grasses and sparkling water peppered with hammocks of cabbage palms. Pelicans and cranes and eagles. Rabbits and raccoons. And alligators.

Yes, the perfect place to disappear.

But the one thing Amber's active imagination could never have conjured, couldn't have predicted, was that SR 50 was the place where *she* would disappear.

As she adjusted her foot on the gas pedal, she felt sand shift between her toes. An hour earlier, she'd been walking on Cocoa Beach, tracing the sparkling moonlight, warm waves lapping over her ankles, a perfect ending to a wonderful weekend.

No, not just wonderful. Life-changing. When her father had suggested that Amber and her brand-new husband, Jonah, pay a visit to renowned local couples therapist Kristen Nogulich, Amber had been more than hesitant.

Heck, on Friday morning Amber had still been dead-set on an annulment.

But Nogulich had been the miracle worker she was touted to be, and Amber had seen that Jonah was the man she'd hoped he was, a man who had overcome his troubles, undone the problems he'd caused. *Her* man. Not the most perfect man in the world, but certainly the most lovable.

She looked at the passenger seat. There was the VHS tape. On the label, in Jonah's big, goofy, kid-like print, was her name—*AMBER*. She smiled, let the warmth of the moment flow over her. Nogulich had them both, in solitude, record "do-over vows," videotaped messages they gave to each other. They hadn't watched them yet. Nogulich said that each person had to hold on to the tape they received until the other person gave permission to watch it.

It had been a long weekend, and Amber's best friend, Kim, the woman who'd been her maid of honor two weeks earlier, extended it even further. After convincing Amber that she should take her father's advice and visit Dr. Nogulich— for which Amber would be forever grateful—Kim had given Amber a solemn offer. She said she would drive to Cocoa Beach, an hour-long trek from Orlando, to meet Amber after her therapy session and walk the beach with her. Some one-on-one time. Girl time. Best friend time. A chance to unload all the emotions that had surely built up in the therapy sessions. Such a kind offer—how in the world could Amber refuse?

But, damn, was she gonna be tired tomorrow...

A quick glance at the clock on the dash. 2:07 a.m. Another forty-five minutes to Orlando. Her shift started at six. With time to get ready and to drive to the dispatch center, that would give her a couple solid hours of sleep. A few drops of Visine—it really does get the red out, after all—

and some cucumbers under the eyes, and she'd be good to go. She could nap in the afternoon.

Nah, things weren't so bad. She had no reason to complain at all, not with things improving so much for her— the newfound understanding of her husband and also the recent turnaround in her father. Both of the men in her life, both of the relationships blossoming at once.

Her father had come so very far recently. Just before the wedding, he'd done the right thing. The right *things*, plural, as a matter of fact.

After all his protestations, after all his insistence that Amber was making a mistake, that she'd chosen a fool, a loser, someone beneath her, he'd finally acquiesced and come to accept Jonah as his future son-in-law. Just in the nick of time.

And her father had also agreed to do the right thing regarding Amber's research. Confronting him had been the hardest thing Amber had ever done. But again she was shocked—and subsequently overjoyed—when her father did the right thing.

There was a spasm in her left thigh, and she took her good hand off the steering wheel for just a moment to massage it. For the longest time, the idea of a wedding ceremony frightened her, the idea of standing in front of a crowd of people, all of them able to see the left side of her body.

Spastic hemiplegic cerebral palsy impaired half of Amber and gave her a slight limp. It had brought her physical discomfort, had shown her the cruelty in the hearts of other human beings, particularly during childhood, and had been an unwelcome defining characteristic.

But it was part of her. So two weeks ago, she strode proudly down the aisle, hobbling, putting the palsy out there, making it visible, front and center.

Her lips pulled open for a yawn, and she brought her right hand up, as though she could stop it. It came out anyway.

She opened her eyes wide and focused on the road ahead, the patch of light on the streaking asphalt. Silver clouds, a large moon, and a spattering of stars decorated a bright and bluish nighttime sky. The swamp was well lit, glowing sapphire shadows, and beside her she could see the shapes of palms and swaying grass, the sparkle of water in the ditch.

She wasn't far outside of Titusville, in Brevard County where the road was called Cheney Highway, so she knew that the land on the right side of the road was St. Johns National Wildlife Refuge, which had been established in 1971 to save the dusky seaside sparrow from extinction. The efforts had failed. The last known individual died at Disney World, of all places, and the species was declared extinct back in '90.

Vanished.

Just like all those poor souls in her dark imaginings moments earlier.

A pair of headlights in the distance ahead. It was the first car she'd seen since she'd turned onto 50 and left civilization behind.

As she continued toward it, something felt off. She squinted, leaning closer to the windshield for a better look.

It wasn't moving. The car was parked diagonally across both lanes on her side of the divided highway. Its headlights blasted across the median and disappeared in the swamp. As she drew closer, she saw that its flashers were on too.

She took her foot from the gas, put it on the brake, flicked on her blinkers.

Two men outside the car. Standing upright and still.

What in the world? It didn't look like there had been an accident. And it certainly wasn't a construction project.

Strange.

Slower yet. Within yards. This close, she could see that the men were looking in her direction. But their mouths were sealed tight, no panic, excitement, or pain on their faces.

A slight flash, something reflected by her headlights.

A gun.

One of them was holding a gun! A shotgun.

No, *both* of them had guns. The second man held a revolver.

Her heart jumped, and her mind instantly flashed to her research, the ramifications she'd worried so much about.

She'd known from the very beginning there could be trouble.

No time to think. She just brought her foot all the way down, smashing the brake pedal. A screech from the tires. The seatbelt cut into her collarbone. Her head went forward, hair flicking into the steering wheel.

And the Bonneville stopped within fifty feet of the parked car. The men looked through her windshield. Their expressions didn't change. They charged toward her.

She threw the gear selector into reverse, gripped the wheel as best she could with her weak left hand, and tossed her other arm over the passenger headrest as she looked back through the rear window. There were shouts from the men, indiscernible.

She jammed her quivering, spasming left hand into a crook of the wheel, against the airbag, and yanked hard. More squealing from the tires. The tangy smell of burnt rubber. A glimpse through the windshield as she turned around. The men were shouting, approaching, aiming their guns.

She listened for the *crack* of a gunshot, the metallic *thump* of a round striking her car, sounds she was certain she would hear.

But they never came.

The Bonneville came to a halt, throwing her against the door. She used her good hand to put it in drive and then smashed the gas pedal. The engine roared. A *chirp* from the tires, and she rocketed off, driving the wrong way on an empty highway, heading back to Titusville.

They hadn't fired. They had guns, they charged her, but they *hadn't* fired. They weren't trying to kill her, then.

She tasted that subtle relief for only a moment before a new realization replaced it.

If they weren't trying to kill her, yet they were armed and blocking her path, what *did* they want?

She pressed harder against the pedal, her calf straining.

A look to the rearview.

The car was following, lights on.

And yet...

She was getting away. Easily. They weren't driving fast. They weren't exactly chasing her, only following.

She couldn't fathom why, but at that moment she was simply thankful that things were working out the way they were.

Maybe she'd escape these men, this sudden, unknown threat.

Then two additional sets of headlights appeared in front of her, flashing into existence so suddenly and so close that it made her scream.

A pair of cars. A quarter mile away. They must have been sitting at the side of the road, parked in one of the rare paths that led off the side of 50 into the wilderness. They flew up the road toward her, one in each lane, blocking her out.

She yanked the wheel to the side and laid on the brakes. The Bonneville shook horribly, its seams and rivets creaking. More of that smell, the sour odor of annihilated tires.

The seatbelt locked and cut into her collarbone, right where it had earlier. Burning. It would leave a mark.

She looked through the windshield. The cars were closing in, braking. She turned. The car behind her was closing in too.

Gasping, she fumbled with the seatbelt. Two attempts. Three. And she got it unlatched. Threw open the door.

Outside. Earthy, moist air. Crickets. Frogs.

Her left leg spasmed, and her knee bent. A hand on the car, its sheet metal slick with humidity, kept her from tumbling over.

The bright sky showed the endless expanse before her. Everything blue and glowing. Spiky palms. A few pine trees. Grasses.

And fortunately, little water. She'd found herself in an area that was mostly dry, aside from the puddle in the ditch.

She bolted down the embankment. Her left leg gave out, and she fell, landing on her shoulder, yelling out.

She rolled, tumbling twice, and splashed into the water.

Her mind went to alligators. She knew what this water looked like in daylight—all green and murky—and her thoughts changed to those of bacterial infections.

She scrambled to her feet, which sank into the mud. Feeling the presence of the men at the road above her, she willed her legs to move, especially the left one, and she splashed out of the water and into the marsh.

Grass. Brushing against her jeans, tickling her hands.

And a palm tree. The only bit of height nearby. She ran toward it.

Car doors slamming shut behind her. Footsteps. Voices.

But still no gunshots.

Her left leg spasmed. Her knee gave out. And she fell again, into the grass.

Damn leg. Goddamn leg!

Her eyes filled with tears. Her stomach roiled.

Focus. Get through this. Think.

The tree. She saw the fronds ahead of her, through the grass. Maybe having fallen wasn't such a bad thing. Now that she was on the ground, she could crawl to the tree and—

No.

No, they had seen her going for the tree. And what kind of plan was that, anyway? What exactly was she going to do once she got there?

She scanned her surroundings. A large indentation in the earth. About ten feet away. Some brush beside it—dried palm fronds, pine branches.

The men would think she'd still be going for the tree. That *had* been her plan, after all, and she had been running that direction when she fell.

They would think she would crawl to the tree, that she would use her fall to her advantage, hiding in the underbrush as she moved.

But she was going for that indentation.

Footsteps closer behind her now. Closing in.

But she could make it. There was just enough time.

Her knees dug into the earth. She clenched the grass with her good hand, using it to pull her to the indentation.

And then she was there.

She rolled herself in, grabbed a hold of the brush, covered herself.

And listened.

Footsteps. Even closer.

Very close.

Approaching.

Within feet of her.

Her lips trembled, and her chest shook. Her leg spasmed.

The footsteps continued on. Growing a bit quieter, a bit more distant.

And stopped. The men were beside the tree.

They'd fallen for the ruse.

A long, mostly quiet moment, punctuated by the small sounds of shifting weight in the underbrush.

The footsteps started again, moving in circles, stomping at an urgent pace. Then they slowed. And there was a voice.

"*Shit!* Where the hell did she go?"

The man's voice frightened her more than anything so far. It wasn't particularly loud or deep or menacing. But it personified the forces that were pursuing her. These were actual *people* who had chased her into the wild.

People who couldn't find her.

She tried to contain her shuddering breaths, which she felt warm and wet against her cheeks, bouncing back upon her from the scratchy palm frond lying on her face.

Slow. Slow the breaths down.

If she could do that, she just might make it out of this.

CHAPTER TWO

Silence Jones stared into the darkness. Somewhere in there was his target.

Somewhere...

But it was so damn dark. Only the tiniest indications of shape, infinitesimal grays.

Then there was a flash. Two minuscule, glistening spots of light, appearing for just a moment. Eyes.

Got you now.

Silence reached out.

And something small and soft and loaded with four razor-sharp points smacked him across the face.

Silence yelled. He instinctively jumped away from the bed, going from a hands-and-knees position to landing on his back. The round area rug absorbed the blow, but his weight brought the rug sliding back on the hardwood floor, and he bashed into the nightstand, his head smacking a drawer handle.

He grunted and put one hand to the back of his head, the other to the wound on his cheek.

A deep, hate-filled, almost prehistoric growl rumbled from beneath the bed.

A moment of grimacing, then Silence took his hand from his cheek, examined it. Two tiny spots of blood.

Baxter's usual temperament was the feline equivalent of Mr. Rogers coming out of heavy sedation. But when a veterinarian visit was in order, the cat transformed into a beast worthy of Roman mythology.

Naturally, on such occasions, Mrs. Enfield called her next-door neighbor for assistance, and Silence dutifully marched over, even though it was a forgone conclusion that Baxter would beat the shit out of him. He simply had to help. Mrs. Enfield—and Baxter, too, for that matter—had been incredibly good to him for years. And one doesn't turn down a blind elderly woman's requests for help.

Silence leaned his head back against the dresser and looked at the bed. The black strip of shadow beneath the box spring taunted him, particularly since the grumbling, popping, sinister growl persisted—one long, unending note.

He took a deep breath, catching a whiff of old lady smell mixed with the scent of the house, which was even older than Mrs. Enfield herself, amazingly enough. It was a nineteenth century beauty, one of many in Pensacola.

Along with his deep breathing, Silence closed his eyes and did a quick meditation. C.C. had taught him the importance of presence. His energy was horrible just then, filled with anger, and there was a frightened animal who needed him. He had to realign.

Looking into the warm nothingness of the inside of his eyes, Silence listened to the ticking of the clock at the bedside, the cat's growling. He sensed his touch points, where his body came into contact with the world around him—the back of his head against the dresser; his hand on his head; his other hand on the hardwood floor; his butt and legs on the wool rug. He envisioned Baxter in his usual state, staring up at Silence with that dumb, pleasant smile and contented eyes bearing a look of sheer admiration, the ever-present line of drool coming from the corner of his mouth, pooling on Silence's thigh.

Silence opened his eyes.

All right, all right.

He pushed himself to his hands and knees and crawled back to the bed, grabbing the bath towel from the floor. He'd brought it with him, but he'd hoped he wouldn't have to use it. Baxter hated being toweled, and he was already stressed enough knowing that he was going to the vet. Silence had made the fool mistake of revealing the plastic carrier crate before having Baxter fully secured. That's how the cat had ended up dug into his stronghold beneath the guest room bed.

But with the wound on his cheek and the appointment time growing nearer and nearer, Silence had no choice but to towel him.

Silence saw the little eyes at the far wall as he crawled. And Baxter saw the towel in his hand.

The growl—which still hadn't broken, a long, continuous sound—suddenly reached an ear-piercing crescendo. And stopped. Baxter hissed.

Silence brought the towel in front of him, scooted his head and broad shoulders under the bed frame as best he could, and made contact with Baxter.

Immediately he felt the cat's strength through the towel. Aside from the fact that Silence was stunned once more by Baxter's ability to change temperament—this was a cat who was rattled by houseflies and lived for scratches behind the ears and marathon naps in the windowsill—Silence also noticed how similar Baxter's sudden strength was to his own. A rigid, taut, wiry, endurance sort of strength. Silence trained

for this, the sort of strength that allowed him to pry open
rusty doors, pull himself up steep embankments, squeeze the
life from a man's throat. But Baxter seemed to have it naturally in some animalistic reserve that he could tap into when-
ever he needed, which was apparently when he had to go to
the veterinarian.

Silence spoke, trying to make his hideous, demonic growl
of a voice as kindly as it could sound. "Come on, Baxter. It's
okay."

It was more syllables than he would typically utter at
once, and it tore his throat up, making his eyes water. But
Baxter was worth it. He was a good boy.

One quick thrust of the hands, and Silence finally had a
good grip on the cat, wrapping the towel fully around him.

He shuffled out from beneath the bed, grabbed the
carrier, threw open its metal gate, and secured the target.

———

The old wooden steps squeaked as Silence descended to the
first floor. Every time he used the staircase—which was rarely,
and more often than not for a Baxter-wrangling mission, as
Mrs. Enfield hardly used the second floor—he felt like some
sort of Southern gentleman of yesteryear. The house was no
mansion, but it had to Silence's mind a very *Gone with the
Wind* vibe with all the ornate Victorian-era touches such as
the exquisite handrail that his fingers traced as he continued
down the steps.

In his other hand was the pet carrier handle. Baxter's
hissing had ceased the moment Silence got him inside, and
since then the cat had been alternating between growls and
scared, pathetic mews. Mostly the latter. Poor guy.

Mrs. Enfield was at the base of the stairs, her milky eyes
looking up, right at the carrier, somehow knowing exactly

where Baxter was. She was small, black, frail, and had hair even whiter than her functionless eyes, from which two lines of tears streamed down the crevices of her wrinkled cheeks.

Knobby knuckles moved in a wave as she rubbed her hands over each other, an infinite loop. She quivered with her sobbing. With her shoulders slouched and her knees bent, she was even tinier than usual, an effect that was amplified by the normal-sized woman standing beside her, wrapping a pair of consoling arms around her.

Lola. Mrs. Enfield's former caretaker. She too was looking up the stairs, but she was looking not at the cat carrier but at Silence. When Silence met her eyes—which were dark and of the Asian variety, the more dominant half of Lola's multiracial heritage—she smiled, motioned toward Mrs. Enfield, and then gave a little shrug of the shoulders that said, *Isn't she cute?*

Silence found nothing cute about Mrs. Enfield's suffering. Sure, this was most likely another false alarm, the latest in a long string of old cat lady vicarious hypochondria. Baxter had been puking for a couple of days, which was more likely from chewing the wrong houseplant than sipping Liquid Plumber. But if Mrs. Enfield felt in her heart of hearts that something was wrong with him, then she was hurting. And that wasn't cute.

He looked away from Lola's gaze.

"You got him!" Mrs. Enfield said, almost shouted, between sobs. "Oh, thank the Lord, you got him!"

"Yes," Silence said.

From the corner of his eye, he saw a slight reaction from Lola. They'd seen each other many times through the years when she came to visit Mrs. Enfield, but upon every new encounter, there was still some sort of involuntary response to his horrendous voice. People couldn't help themselves; the voice was *that* jarring.

He stepped up to the women, raised the carrier a few

inches to Mrs. Enfield's height so that Baxter could see her and she could sense him.

"Hi, Si," Lola said in a tone too upbeat for the situation. She was a good caretaker, though, and she continued to rub Mrs. Enfield's shoulders even while looking at Silence.

"Hi."

She'd called him Si. Mrs. Enfield called him Si, a nickname of familiar endearment, and she'd passed it on to Lola.

The old woman had a finger halfway in the carrier, and Baxter rubbed against it.

"It'll be okay, baby," she said as she ran her fingertip along the wet part of Baxter's nose.

"Nice of you to come over," Lola said, rubbing her hand over Mrs. Enfield's shoulder after a fresh wave of tears but still looking at Silence. "You're lucky I'm visiting, or you'd be the one taking her to the vet."

She leaned closer to Mrs. Enfield.

"It's time for us to go, ma'am."

A moan from the old woman, hands going to her face.

"Will be all right," Silence said.

Lola took the carrier from Silence, their hands brushing on the handle. A sudden laugh as she looked past Silence.

He turned, but he already knew what she was looking at.

That damn photograph.

It sat in a pewter frame on a small accent table near the base of the stairs. To Silence, it felt like the photo had been taken yesterday, but as he thought about it, it had been over three *years*.

Lola had taken the photo. At Mrs. Enfield's request. Silence, sitting upright in a hideous old wooden chair, one of many items in Mrs. Enfield's house that looked like it had been yanked straight out of a horror movie. On Silence's lap was Baxter, looking at the camera, head twisted just so, the biggest goddamn cat smile you've ever seen in your life, a steady line of drool draining from the lower corner of his mouth, a puddle of it clearly visible on Silence's pants, which he remembered were one of his favorite pairs of Calvin Kleins at the time.

Silence, too, was looking at the camera. And smiling. He rarely smiled and never did so on command, so the expression would have been unnatural enough had his mind not also been both toying with the humiliating awkwardness of the situation and wondering why the hell he was being forced to pose for a photo for a blind woman. The resulting look on Silence's face was one of pain, bewilderment, and despair, something truly hideous, something that would scare small children and wilt perfectly healthy fields of crops. Just absolutely hideous.

And it made Lola break into hysterics every time she came to Pensacola to visit her former employer.

She kept a hand on Mrs. Enfield's shoulder as she bent over, folding at the waist, the knees. Her laughter turned so intense it went silent.

"You're looking at the picture again, aren't you?" Mrs. Enfield said. Her white eyes roamed her immediate surroundings, drifting over Silence to Lola, bent over beside her. She sniffed. And a small smile came to her lips, the first all morning.

When Lola couldn't respond, Silence answered for her. "She is."

"Now you stop it." The old woman stepped out of Lola's hand and padded to the table, picked up the frame, held it gingerly, squeezed it to her bosom. "It's a beautiful photo. My two boys."

"You can't see," Silence said.

"*Stop it!* Both of you. I was there when she took it. I know what it shows."

Lola finally straightened up. Her laughter became audible

again. She wiped tears from her eyes, took a deep breath, sighed.

"Come on, Mrs. E." She stepped over and took Mrs. Enfield's hand. "Let's go."

———————

Outside, the temperature was pleasant, but the sun was hot, the humidity high. Willinger Street was one of many quiet streets in Pensacola's East Hill neighborhood, full of historic homes, well-kept gardens, and children on bicycles. Lola's Ford Taurus was parked right in front of the house, and once she'd seat-belted Baxter's carrier in the back seat and Mrs. Enfield in the front, she closed the door and stepped to Silence.

"I'll take good care of her."

"Thanks."

"Tonight's my last night in town..." She left it dangling. Not unfinished. Just open.

"Okay."

She knew Silence was engaged. That's what Mrs. Enfield had always told her. That's what Silence had always told her. And in Silence's mind, it was true.

But through the years, Lola had noticed that Silence never got married, that his fiancée was never around. Mrs. Enfield hadn't told her that C.C. was dead, and neither had Silence. And while Lola had never expressly asked him out, she was more friendly to him than she should be to an engaged man.

She looked at him. Waiting.

BEEP!

His pager sounded.

Thank god.

He pulled it from his pocket, squinted at the screen,

perhaps a bit too dramatically, then gave Lola a *Work, Whatcha gonna do?* shrug and left for his house.

"Bye," she called behind him.

He turned. She stood where he'd left her, a few feet from the Taurus.

He waved.

———

When he dialed the number that had beeped him, the voice that responded didn't say hello. Nor did it offer any other word of salutation. Rather, the greeting was a laugh—a big, hearty belly laugh, the kind of laugh that belts across a restaurant or an airport terminal upon the reunion of two buddies who haven't seen each other in years. It was a man who went by Falcon but whose actual name was Laswell. Silence's boss, a higher-up in the Watchers. And it had been less than three weeks since they'd spoken.

"*Hahaaaaaaa!*" Falcon shouted. Silence pulled the phone from his ear. "Si, how you doin', you big, dog-voiced son of a bitch?"

Like Mrs. Enfield, Falcon had chosen to shorten Silence's name to Si.

"Good. You?"

"I'm doing great. Just great. Thanks for asking, *amigo*. The sun's shining here in whatever state it is I live in." Silence wasn't permitted to know Falcon's location, occupation, or even his real name, though Silence had figured that last one out. "Meatloaf's on the menu tonight. And I have a hell of a juicy assignment for my Florida man. You ready for this?"

"Yes."

"Orlando. Two months ago a newlywed woman disappeared a couple weeks after the wedding. Amber Lund. She was driving home from couple's therapy." He chuckled.

"Therapy after two weeks of marriage—love must not've been in the air. Car was found at the side of a highway a couple of miles from a bus station. Of course, the immediate assumption was she got retroactive cold feet, that something big came up in the therapy sessions and she ran off to cope with it, hopped on a bus and got the hell out of Dodge.

"But here's the thing—highway patrol didn't even search for a full week. Since then, the husband has insisted that people continue to look for her, but the father has been fighting it, saying that the husband's a loser, that his daughter surely had second thoughts and is out there somewhere in the great wide open finding herself, that's why no one's heard from her in two months.

"The dad's a former Orlando police officer, worked for a district known for corruption, multiple internal affair investigations spanning decades, from which nothing ever materialized. Seems an awfully weird coincidence. My thought is that the district is so corrupt that people get caught in the crossfire. Family members. Like Amber. Could be retaliation, a planned hit from someone the district pissed off, which would explain why the search was called off so abruptly, why the dad's so quick to brush it off—can't have people digging too deep into the district's dirty business.

"Sounds like somebody needs some killin'. That's where you come in. Figure out what the hell happened to this girl. Eliminate those who need it. Details coming momentarily. Questions?"

"No."

"Good luck, Suppressor."

Click.

He was gone. The next time Silence would hear from him would be the next time Silence needed to do "some killin'." Which would be sooner than later.

Silence put the phone back in the cradle.

There was a beep from one of the bedrooms. His fax machine.

The boards of the old home creaked as he walked to the back. The house wasn't old in the same way as Mrs. Enfield's —his was a leftover from the post-war boom, much newer— but it bellyached nearly as much as hers.

Silence waited next to the machine, which sat on a small table by the window. It buzzed as it worked, huffing out plasticky-smelling heat, warming Silence's arm. Papers stacked up in the output tray as they printed. When the last sheet fell into place, there was a final screech of communication through the phone line.

Finished.

He picked up the stack.

On top was a brief note from Falcon, the same information he'd given over the phone, with a final sentence stating:

I'm rootin' for ya.

Sincerely,
Your Biggest Fan
XOXOXO

Falcon enjoyed making light of the relatively short life expectancy Silence enjoyed as an Asset, one of the Watchers' field agents.

Photocopied newspaper articles followed Falcon's initial note.

New Bride Feared Missing

Lund Search Continues

Search Called off for Missing Orlando Woman

Husband Pleads for More Resources in Private Search for Missing Woman

Following the articles were two pages of biographical information on the three individuals the Watchers had deemed to be pertinent to the case—Amber Lund; her father, Carlton Stokes; and her husband, Jonah Lund. The information had been mined via the Watchers' considerable talent hidden in plain sight within all levels of U.S. bureaucracy.

The last pages were photos of the three people. Some were scans from newspapers while several of the photos of Carlton Stokes and Jonah Lund had clearly been taken surreptitiously—candid images of them leaving buildings, ordering coffees, crossing parking lots. Commissioned photographs taken by a private detective.

Silence picked up a photograph of Stokes, one of the spy pics. White, early sixties. Silver-and-black hair, medium length, with sideburns. Dark eyebrows over a generous nose and a long, slightly jowly face. Silence could easily put this guy's image behind a desk in a 1980s cop movie, have him fill the cranky ol' lieutenant role. *You're a loose cannon! I'm gonna have your gun and badge after this latest stunt you've pulled!* Knowing that Stokes was a former police officer perhaps informed the fantasy.

He flipped to another of the commissioned photos, this one of Jonah Lund. He was walking down a sidewalk in what must have been downtown Orlando, head down, hands shoved in his pockets. An open green flannel over a black T-shirt. Jeans. Sunglasses. White, twenties, average build.

Another photo of Jonah Lund, one of the newspaper photos, clearly taken long before losing his wife, a snapshot, happy times. He wore a different flannel over a different T-shirt and a casual, lopsided smile that twisted up a corner of his face, the sort of smile that had surely been a factor in winning Amber's heart. Dark brown hair coifed. Slight cleft to his chin. A guy brimming with the breezy confidence of youth, grasping life firmly by the balls.

Silence waited to view Amber Lund's image last. In Silence's line of work, it was always difficult dealing with missing persons. It would be a challenge under any circumstances, but with the cases Silence worked, there was always something hideous involved.

Always.

He was an assassin, after all.

So when a person was missing, this invariably meant something awful was happening or had happened to the individual. The best-case scenario, sadly enough, was that the person was being held for ransom.

Or the person might be raped.

Or sold into human trafficking.

Or tortured.

Or dead.

That's why he hesitated before flipping to a photo of Amber Lund.

It was a newspaper photo, a snapshot like the one of her husband. Sitting at a wrought-iron table outside a restaurant or café or coffee shop. Laughing. Sunglasses perched atop her head, consumed by blonde hair. Thin. Heart-shaped face. Slightly wide-set eyes under a slightly tall forehead. At a casual glance, someone might see simply the latest blonde-haired, blue-eyed perfection. But there was a lot more to Amber Lund. Silence could see it.

Some people viewed others only in shades of the apparent, but Silence could see more, into the depths of those around him. C.C. had told him he was empathic, that he could see people's souls, their auras. Silence wasn't spiritual in the same way as C.C.—his ethereal, kindly, bohemian beauty —but he recognized that he had a mostly accurate ability to sense a person's character upon sight, even from a photograph.

And in Amber Lund, Silence saw deep humanity. One hell of a soul. She radiated it. The biographical information noted that she had cerebral palsy. Silence had observed that afflictions like this often left people with a deeper appreciation, some sort of stronger tie to the purer core of all that was, a glimpse behind the veil at the simplicity of the magic. What some might see as a curse often ended up being a blessing.

One more glance at her photo, then he stuck it back in the stack.

Time to begin.

CHAPTER THREE

A CITY BUS.

As Finley sat down on the thin, cheap cushion, he could almost feel the embedded grime work its way through his pants, the back of his shirt. The chrome pole beside him—which he refused to touch—was slick with the oils of a thousand hands, finger- and palm prints smeared into a wavy, blotchy mess. His shoes stuck to the floor.

The bright, ugly lighting revealed dust mushrooming up from his soft impact against the seat. And it also revealed a lot of ugly people. Fat people and smelly people and working people and happy people and sad people. More sad than happy.

But the only person who mattered was the one in the back, the one staring at him—Guzman, the reason Finley had found himself entombed in this rolling shithole cocoon of rotting humanity. The organization had offered Finley a second chance, and one that he was incredibly grateful for. But gratitude and humbleness weren't equivalent to lowering oneself. Finley had worked damn hard to get away from things like city buses and dive motels and cheap discount stores with flickering lights, the smell of cigarette-drenched clothing, slightly damaged goods, and grimy floors.

He took his eyes off Guzman for just a moment, looked down, at his shoes, a nice pair of Doc Martens that he'd paid full price for at a nice store. Fashionable, trendy, but rugged enough for the sort of work he did. He moved his left foot. *Crrrruff* as the floor stuck to the thick rubber sole.

Finley sighed inwardly.

You're here for a job. It's not your life.

A job. A second chance. The best opportunity he'd ever gotten. He'd damn well better get his head on straight.

He looked up at Guzman. Found his eyes already staring at him.

Fear looking right into Finley from smallish, wide-set eyes. Guzman had surely thought he'd gotten free—Finley had kept his distance for twenty minutes after momentarily losing track of the guy back at the parking lot—and this bus was going to take Guzman to the depot and out of town.

That's why Finley had strolled so casually onto the bus, as much as he detested doing so. That's why he'd sat in plain sight of the man, locking eyes with him as he sat down. Guzman needed to see how easy it had been, how little chance there was of escape.

Guzman would no longer be getting off at the depot where the line terminated. He would get off at the next stop and try to escape into the darkness. Hell, Finley was surprised that Guzman hadn't pulled the bus's stop-request cord, thrown open the doors as they slid apart, and dashed off.

Guzman was the shape of a potato and short. Dark, thinning hair. A compressed face too small for his head, leaving lots of extra skin at the sides. Dirty sneakers. Jeans and a clever print T-shirt bearing an industrial-style warning sign— *CAUTION: STAY BACK 25 FEET. HAVEN'T HAD MY COFFEE YET.*

Hilarious…

Finley would enjoy this.

The metallic squeal of brakes, piercing, an unpleasant punctuation to an unpleasant experience. Everything shifted forward. Finley refused to grab the grimy pole beside him. He kept his eyes locked on Guzman.

The bus stopped. Several people stood. And, as predicted, Guzman bolted for the rear door. He shoved his way past a woman—who barked at him—and was the first person out of the bus.

Finley stood and waited at the front door. Two people in front of him. No rush. There was no need.

Outside. A less-than-wonderful area of town. A McDonald's across the street. The smell of day-old grease. Steamy windows. Teenagers loitering by the doors. Laughter and shouts echoing in the distance, a few conversations nearby from the others leaving the bus, all of it sounding as hopeless as the surroundings.

Guzman would have considered going into the McDonald's, losing himself in the late-night crowd, maybe going to the bathroom with the plan of hiding in a stall for a couple of hours, sitting on the toilet with his knees pulled to his face, hiding his feet from view. But he would have decided against it, felt it foolish.

Finley had been dealing with Guzman long enough to know how the slimeball's mind worked. Guzman would have gone for the dark alley behind the McDonald's.

Finley walked past the reek of the overfilled dumpster, around a fence, and to the alley.

Yep. There he was. Crossing the backyard of one of the houses bordering the alley, clinging to a line of shadows that edged a patch of illumination from the floodlight on the house's deck.

Finley whistled.

Guzman stopped. Looked back.

"Oh, shit!"

Finley dashed toward him, his Doc Martens gripping into the wet, overgrown weeds of the backyard, through the light and to the shadow. He caught Guzman by the back of his clever, sweat-soaked T-shirt and pulled him back.

Guzman took a swing, which Finley casually turned to avoid. He used the creep's new position to his advantage, wrapping Guzman's arm around his own body, tying him up.

A sound to the right. The sliding glass door at the back of the house. Opening.

With one hand on Guzman's arm, Finley used the other to grab hold of the man's jeans and rolled him over the short wooden fence. Then he hopped the fence himself.

He crouched beside Guzman in the scraggly, forsaken plants running along the fence in the neighbor's yard, which was perfectly dark, no exterior lights, no light coming from the windows.

He gave Guzman a *shut up* look. Guzman remained quiet, his tiny eyes looking up at him, having reached their full scope.

Footsteps in the yard beside them. They came a few feet away from the glass door, seemingly in Finley's direction, but quickly went the opposite way, back to the house, followed by dumb-sounding muttering, "Gawd damn it." The sliding door shut.

Finley reached under his sport jacket, took his Smith & Wesson 4506 from its shoulder holster, put it to Guzman's sweaty temple.

The small eyes closed. The lips turned down into a cartoon-perfect frown and trembled along with the rest of him. He raised his hands.

Finley didn't need to say much. These situations required no communication. There was never a fraction of uncertainty in a mark's mind about why he'd been marked, why he'd been hunted and caught. They always knew.

So Finley just said, "Six hundred dollars."

"I ... I don't..."

Sobbing.

Finley patted him down, his hand slapping against Guzman's soft flesh, which jiggled. A small pistol in his back pocket. Finley transferred it to his own. Then he holstered his Smith, slapped a hand over Guzman's wet mouth, and brought a fist hard into his stomach.

Guzman squealed. Finley felt it through his fingers.

"Eight hundred, then. Tomorrow."

Another fist to his stomach. Harder.

"Eight hundred, asshole! Have it tomorrow."

Another punch. Another. Again and again. Driving his fist into Guzman's doughy stomach. Blood trickled between Finley's fingers, mixed with spit and sweat and tears. Soon Guzman would be pissing blood as well. Maybe shitting it.

Finley stopped. He stood up.

"Eight hundred."

He eyed the spot in the center of the stomach where he'd been punching, used it as a bullseye, lined up a vicious kick—

And the cellular phone in his pocket rang.

———

Back outside the McDonald's, at the sidewalk, under a streetlight, a few feet away from the restaurant's outdoor playground, its menagerie of wooden structures and slides and swing sets inhabited by three stumbling, grown-ass men in baggy pants and gold chains, drunk at six in the morning.

He'd left Guzman in a weeping, crippled pile in the yard and walked a few feet away to somewhere he could return the call. He would have preferred getting the hell away from this decrepit part of the city, but his employer was not the kind of person you kept waiting. And there was no way in hell Finley was going to jeopardize his opportunity, this life he'd been afforded.

"Sir," he said when his employer answered.

His employer inquired as to his whereabouts.

"Somewhere on the west side. Guzman, sir. He needed a little encouragement. It'll be eight hundred tomorrow. Or I'll terminate the account. My thought is—"

His employer had a different matter to discuss, wanted him elsewhere.

"But Guzman—"

His employer didn't care about Guzman. There was something much more pressing.

Finley's eyes widened as he listened. And before he replied, he was already moving, heading in the direction he needed to go.

He had to get there damn fast.

"I'll be right there, sir."

CHAPTER FOUR

PEOPLE DO CONFOUNDING, even counterintuitive things during times of high pressure, Jonah Lund assured himself. *Desperate times call for desperate measures*, as they say. But he was still rather amazed at himself—he'd let this large, intimidating-looking man into his apartment!

Jonah stared at the plastic business card in his hand, which the man had handed him wordlessly when Jonah answered the door. He squinted at it as much to decipher the reality of the situation as to question the credibility of the text.

Jonah held it in both hands, and he rubbed his thumbs along the rounded corners. The plastic was clear but frosted with a matte finish. The ink was thick, raised off the surface, dark blue, glossy. Simple but stately blue stripes on the left side. It was the sort of card you expected from a Wall Street trader, an elite real estate agent, an embellishing piece of flair that says, *See? I'm so successful I can spend a dollar per business card.*

But this card had been completely repurposed. Where there would normally be a company logo, a name, an address, a phone number, maybe even an email address, there was just the strange message.

And its owner wanted it back. The man held out a hand.

Jonah reached across the coffee table and gave it to him. The sharp cuts of the man's jaw and cheekbones and chin along with his piercing dark eyes said fashion model, but the professional air, the assertiveness, and the look of quiet compassion while he patiently waited on Jonah to finish examining his card said something else.

He was tall, about six-foot-three, and he dwarfed Jonah's rather small armchair—part of Jonah's entry-level set that the lady at Rooms To Go had assured him would look larger in his apartment, furniture that would soon have been a memory when he and Amber bought their first house. The man's pale gray V-neck shirt had a bit of sheen, and it looked brand-new and expensive. The bit of the man's chest that showed at the shirt's V was taut and hard, striations rippling at the edges. He wasn't bulky, but he was muscular as all hell. He wore a pair of dark gray pants and a dark sport coat over the V-neck.

Jonah leaned back in his seat. "So I don't understand how ... You ... you're here to help me?"

The man nodded.

"And you *can* speak, only limitedly?"

"Yes."

Jonah jumped back in his seat. The man's voice sounded like it came from the depths of his belly, forced through stratifying layers of rock before leaving his mouth. That one word, one syllable, *Yes*, had been a small equation of sounds, rumbling and hissing and popping.

It was so startling that for a moment, Jonah didn't reply. The man just looked at him, unfazed, waiting.

"What's your name?" Jonah said.

"Brett."

Another syllable, another crackling growl. This time, though, the man also gave him a slight rise at the corner of his mouth, a tiny, communicative grin.

He didn't look like a Brett.

"Your name's not really Brett, is it? You're not going to tell me who you really are or who you work for."

He shook his head.

"Government?"

He shook his head.

"Why should I trust you?"

He shrugged.

Jonah breathed in. Held it. Sighed it out. Whoever this man was—whoever Brett was—he was the only person in a month who'd offered to help. And Jonah needed help. He was all by himself.

He stared at Brett for a while longer. The refrigerator a few feet away hummed. Brett blinked.

Jonah crossed his arms over his knees. "How do we begin?"

"Talk," Brett said.

The word was as gentle, as kindly sounding as could be expected from his demonic voice.

"Since you're here to help, I'm guessing you know the situation—that Amber disappeared and I'm the husband who won't let the story die, who thinks she's still out there in the marshes, while her father is convinced I'm a loser and Amber's just run off from me."

Brett nodded.

"What the papers didn't tell you is that her father, Carlton, hates me for a good reason." He looked to the faux wood laminate floorboards. "I cheated on Amber."

He glanced up at Brett, waited for a reaction. Nothing, just a blink.

"I didn't tell her until a few months into the engagement. So at first she didn't know if she was gonna go through with the wedding. And then after the wedding there was new contention, which is why we went to the couples therapy."

"You told her?" Brett said and stopped to swallow. A small grimace. "Or she found out?"

"I confessed to her. I may seem like a real scumbag to you now, but I did truly love her. The cheating wasn't that important. I mean, if it was only a few months after we started dating, and we'd been together for years afterward, what did it really matter?" He looked Brett over, expecting condemnation. The face was still blank. "But I couldn't marry her and keep the secret."

He took one of the remote controls off the glass coffee

table that sat between them, watched it move as he twisted it in his hands.

"I want you to know that Carlton *always* hated me, from the very beginning, before the cheating. Said I was pitiful, that Amber could do better than a guy who worked at a coffee shop. A year later, me and my buddy *owned* the coffee shop—Roast and Relax, downtown. Didn't matter to Carlton. Still a loser in his eyes. Then, of course, Amber told him about the cheating shortly before the wedding. And after the new ... um, contention surfaced, it was Carlton's idea that we go to the couples therapist, Dr. Nogulich, an expert he'd heard about. Carlton tried to swoop in after treating her like shit her entire life, take on the sanctimonious role at the expense of his daughter's loser husband."

"Explain," Brett said.

"Amber had cerebral palsy." He stopped. He'd said *had*. Amber *had* cerebral palsy. Past tense. Even though he'd made peace with it, the sound of it was still abrasive. "It was slight but very much a part of her. A limp, poor function in the left side of her body. She was never good enough for Carlton, flawed, always trying to prove herself to him."

Brett cocked his head slightly.

"I'm serious, man," Jonah said. "What kind of father wouldn't want the search for his daughter to continue as long as possible? I'm telling you, he didn't give a shit about her, and her disappearance is because of the police district he worked in when he was a cop, District C11. Shady stuff goes down there—corruption, internal affairs investigations. And I think Amber was a victim of it all, years after Carlton retired, some old grudge, somebody getting payback. Carlton's holding a press conference later, at the police headquarters downtown." He looked at the clock. "In two hours. Trying to discredit me once and for all."

"We go," Brett said.

"To the press conference?"

Brett nodded.

Jonah hesitated. "Okay."

Great. Just great. Gonna go to the press conference where everyone would recognize him and where he would be persona non grata, at least in the eyes of those supporting the man throwing the conference.

"Carlton will double down on his narrative—that Amber is out there somewhere, off the grid, finding herself after the couples therapy finally revealed to her what a loser her new husband is, what a huge mistake she made. But I'm gonna keep fighting him. More private searches in the swamp. We need to find her. *I* need to find her. I've already made my peace, but I need ... closure."

Brett raised an eyebrow.

"Yes, closure. I know she's dead. I just feel it. If I don't seem as depressed as you would have thought, that's why. I've already been mourning for two months. My wife's dead. Have you ever known someone so deeply, been so connected that you can just ... feel it?"

Brett didn't reply, but Jonah could tell he'd struck a chord. The man's expression lost a tiny bit of its neutrality, cheeks sinking, eyes expanding a fraction.

"She's dead. Another victim of District C11. She'd been working on something this past year, some sort of research project, she called it. Wouldn't tell me what it was. She began shortly after I told her about the cheating. She wasn't a vindictive type, not in the slightest, but she said I had no right to pry into her business after the secret I had kept from her. She said she'd tell me about it eventually, after she was finished.

"I think she was investigating C11. See, she worked as a police dispatcher, trying to win Carlton's respect, one of the few ways a person with palsy could work for the police. I think she started looking into things at the dispatch center, what resources she had available to her there, and something sparked, put her on this quest. It might have been some wish fulfillment too. Her childhood dream was to be a detective.

"So when she moved all her stuff in a couple months ago, our plan was to run out the lease here while we searched for a house. She took over the second bedroom, transferred the office from her old apartment, had the place covered with sticky notes, made me promise to not look at anything, that her investigation was important and she'd share everything with me when it was over. When the cops came, they took all her stuff, but I found this. It had slid between the baseboard and the wall."

He handed Brett a pink sticky note that said:

Weasel
407-555-2822

"Weasel?" Brett said.

"Your guess is as good as mine."

Brett pointed at the number. "Called?"

"Yeah, I called. Got a disconnect notice."

Brett regarded the note. A long moment. Then he placed it on his thigh.

Jonah hadn't meant for Brett to keep it.

Brett looked away, thinking. And his eyes brightened fractionally.

"TCB," he said.

"Huh?"

Brett pointed.

Ah. The poster.

A black-and-white advertisement for BTO's second album, 1973's *Bachman-Turner Overdrive II*. It featured an image of the LP, a gearshift thrusting out of its center, and emblazoned at the top was, "BACHMAN-TURNER OVER-DRIVE IS PULLING AWAY."

The album featured BTO's hit song, "Takin' Care of Business," sometimes shortened to TCB, as Brett had called it.

Jonah grinned. "'Takin' Care of Business,' yeah. Gotta love the classics."

There was the tiniest lifting at the corners of Brett's mouth.

He was human, after all.

"There's also this," Jonah said and reached to the lower of the two tiers of the coffee table, grabbed the VHS tape which bore another sticky note, a classic yellow one, with his name written in Amber's handwriting—*JONAH*.

"When we went to the couples therapy, the doctor had us record new vows. Do-over vows. We gave the tapes to each other, but we weren't to watch them until the other person said we could. Amber hadn't told me I could watch it yet. Like I said, I know in my heart that she's passed, but I still can't bring myself to watch it. Here." He handed the tape to Brett along with the remote he'd been fiddling with. He grabbed the other remote, the one for the VCR, and handed it to him as well. "Probably just personal stuff, but there might be something relevant for us. You never know. I'll go to the other room for a few."

———

After ten minutes of afternoon television—a smutty talk show featuring a disturbed family from Ohio screaming at each other while the host tried to maintain a semblance of control—Jonah muted the twenty-inch TV on the nightstand. He stepped to the closed door, put his ear to it, listened hesitantly. Had Brett watched the tape yet? He couldn't hear Amber's voice, and he didn't want to.

No sounds from the other side of the apartment.

He did smell something, though, coming not from the hallway but from the room he was in. Stale, earthy, musty. The odor of seldom-washed sheets and a pile of dirty clothes in the corner by the vertical blinds covering the sliding glass doors that led to the balcony. The odor of arrested development. The bedroom had that smell for two years. Amber moved in for two weeks, and it vanished. And for two months since, the smell had returned.

He pressed his ear to the door again and listened. A voice. But not Amber's. A deep, crackling voice. With pauses. Brett was on the phone.

Jonah went down the hall, found Brett using a cellular, sitting where he'd left him, the television behind him showing the VCR's bright blue standby screen. Brett was hunched over the coffee table, writing on a small notebook.

For a moment, it looked to Jonah like Brett was drawing something, which was perplexing. Then Jonah saw that he wasn't drawing but making small circles. He was mind mapping, a technique Jonah had learned in college—a means of visually organizing information.

"Yes, sir," Brett said and collapsed the phone, put it in his pocket.

Jonah pointed to the TV. "Well?"

Brett shook his head. "But there's this."

Brett flipped back a page on his notebook, picked it up, held it out for Jonah.

On an otherwise blank page, Brett had written, *Morrison Mission, 399 Roland Street.* Stuck on the page beneath Brett's notation was Amber's pink sticky note.

"Old number," Brett said and put his finger to the phone number Amber had written. "Homeless shelter."

"How did you figure that out?"

Brett traced his finger up from the sticky note to the address he'd written. "Let's go."

He snapped the notebook shut, stood, and headed for the door.

Jonah remained where he was for a moment, then chased after him.

Well, okay then.

CHAPTER FIVE

A FIERO.

Silence hadn't been in one of these for a while. A bit of a modern automotive classic, an icon of the previous decade. Did anything say 1980s more than a Pontiac Fiero?

Jonah hadn't destroyed the car—the thick, sticky shine of Armor All on the dash proved he did spruce it up from time to time—but the stained seats, littered floor, and mildew smell said that the machine's future didn't lie in a car museum.

Silence was riding shotgun. He would let the local do the driving, leave his rental car at the apartment complex. He'd long ago abandoned petty pissing-match competitions of choosing who got to be behind the wheel. Now he based the decision on expedience. It was efficient. C.C. had always told him to work smart, not hard.

Jonah fired up the engine, which came to life with a belch and a stench. He then peered up, through the windshield, at the sky. In typical Florida fashion, the weather had done a quick change, the sunlight now replaced by a swirling gray sky, ready to spit rain at any moment.

Jonah grabbed the shift knob and began to release the clutch, but before they could move, Silence spoke. There was something he needed to know, and he needed to know now, before they made another move.

"Contention?" he said.

Jonah turned. "Huh?"

Silence motioned toward the apartment. "You said, 'contention.'" He swallowed, lubricating his throat for a few more words. "With Amber." Another swallow. "Reason for couples therapy."

Jonah's fingers twitched on the shift knob, which was smeared with black goo—more excess Armor All, dirtied by hand grime. A long inhale whistled through his teeth, a hesitant breath that would surely precede resistance.

Silence countered with preemptive insistence. "Must know." And when Jonah still hesitated, he added, "You must be open."

Jonah looked down at his fingers on the shift knob. Bit his lip. Then he put the car in neutral and pulled up the parking brake, on the left side of the driver's seat, by the door.

His forearms went to the top of the steering wheel, which he'd wrapped with perforated vinyl, secured by a thin, matching vinyl cord, one of those cheap kits you pick up at a discount store. He put his chin on his arm, looking up into the gray sky again.

"When I first told Amber I cheated on her, I said it had happened within the first few months. She came to grips with it; we got married. Then the guilt got to me a couple weeks later. I had to tell her the real truth." He bit his lip, and his eyes searched higher into the sky as they filled with tears. "I didn't cheat on her within the first few months. I lied about that part. It happened years after we'd started dating. It was ... Oh, shit, man. It was only eight months ago."

Silence didn't reply.

Jonah exhaled. A patch of vapor bloomed and quickly vanished on the windshield. The Fiero's engine idled. It had a slight knock.

A long moment passed, then Jonah suddenly jolted off the wheel, turned to Silence, a look of retaliation.

"Once, man. Just once. Stupidest goddamn mistake I've ever made. I'm sure you've pulled some bonehead goofs, right? We got a liquor license at Roast and Relax about a year and a half ago, started with wine, craft beer, mimosas on Sunday mornings. But eventually the nighttime turned into more of a bar vibe. I was working, my shift ended early, about eight. I'd served this girl a few glasses of Moscato. She'd been flirty, wanted to buy me a drink when my shift was over. I let it go too far. I had a few beers..."

He stopped, took a breath.

"I was pretty drunk. But not *that* drunk. Not drunk enough for what I did. Took a taxi to her place. Banged the shit out of her. I wish I could say that I was horribly drunk, that Amber and I had been fighting. No. I was perfectly within my capacities, and Amber and I hardly ever fought. She was goddamn *perfect!* So of course I had to tell her what I did. Who wouldn't tell someone like her? She was a pure soul. I just didn't have the balls to tell her the whole truth."

He blinked faster, leaned his head back farther. A few deep breaths.

"But it gets worse, if you can believe that. A lot worse. Horrendous." Another deep breath. "After I cheated on her, I rationalized it. I actually had the gall to tell myself it was okay because ... Oh, shit."

Another pause to recompose. His breathing had gone supersonic, damn near hyperventilating.

"Because Amber couldn't do everything, you know? Physically. Due to her condition."

A sick feeling came to Silence's stomach.

"Told her that too?" Silence said.

This made Jonah gasp. One of the tears that he'd been fighting to contain fell down his cheek. He wiped it away.

"Yes, goddamn it. I told her that too. I ... I shouldn't have. Shouldn't have told her that part. Don't know why I did. I didn't say it angrily. I didn't say it when I was defending myself. I just ... said it."

Jonah's chin dropped. He nodded. Then shook his head. Then nodded again. The inward tangling of disgust displaying itself in binary.

Silence looked away, downward, between his shoes, at the dark stain on the floor mat.

Shit.

Maybe this investigation was a whole hell of a lot less complicated than Falcon and the Watchers' fact-finders had anticipated. Maybe the fact that the police called off the search abruptly had nothing to do with dirty politics among crooked cops.

Because if Silence were a betting man, he'd say that a seemingly amazing woman had a coming-to-her-senses moment after the man she'd just married admitted to being a goddamn liar who, only months prior, "banged the shit out of" another woman because of Amber's physical handicap.

Silence would place a bet that Amber had run off to do some soul-searching.

Just like her father had said.

And if—

"Hey," Jonah said.

Silence turned, found Jonah scowling at him.

"Now you believe him, don't you?" Jonah said. "You believe Carlton. You think he's right, that Amber left the loser, cheating, lying husband behind to go find herself."

Silence didn't reply.

"You do. I can see it in your eyes. Shit, man, I thought you were here to help."

Jonah's nostrils flared, the lines of his forehead oscillating between anger and pain. When Silence said nothing in response, Jonah's facial mutations slowed, halting at pain.

His arms returned to the steering wheel, and his gaze returned to the gray sky. "It was a choice. A horrible freaking choice. And now I'm paying for it. Forever. This is my life now. Ya know, there are always going to be things that come along in life, blindside you, but those only count for so much before responsibility comes roaring back in. At the end of the day, we design our own lives through the choices we make."

Silence couldn't agree more. And as with most words of poignancy, Jonah's musings brought forth a connection in Silence's mind to the event.

C.C.'s murder had come out of nowhere. It had "blind-sided" him, as Jonah had put it.

But then choices were made, and the responsibility that Jonah mentioned became apparent.

Silence's former self had made the *choice* to seek bloody revenge.

He remembered the horrible, sickening fog that had enveloped him. The way he'd stumbled about in a constant state of lightheadedness, nausea, headache, tears.

One could easily blame that fog for what happened. "Temporary insanity," a lawyer might call it.

But Silence took full responsibility for the choices.

The choice he'd made to stalk them down.

The choice to snap necks.

The choice to look into pleading, weeping eyes and place a bullet between them, warm blood splattering his arms, his face, squinting his eyes.

And, as Jonah said, those choices had designed his life. Along with a little more of that blindside fate, his choices had cost him his voice, his prior face, his prior identity, and his freedom.

He'd have it no other way.

The revenge had been worth it.

It had been his choice.

Jonah took a deep breath and leaned back in the driver's seat, faced Silence again.

"Should I watch it?" he said and reached into the large front pocket of his Baja jacket—blue-and-gray-striped, nice and clean and cozy, not a genuine hemp "drug rug" but something purchased at a shopping mall—and brought forth the VHS tape bearing a sticky note with his name written in his wife's hand.

Silence hadn't noticed that he'd brought the tape with him. It was such an odd thing to do, carrying it with him in his jacket, that it made Silence wonder if Jonah brought it with him everywhere.

As a reply, Silence only gave a shrug.

This wasn't Silence's area of expertise, consoling a brand-new acquaintance. Jonah's decision of whether or not to watch Amber's do-over vows was entirely his own.

His choice.

Silence's mind flashed to what Jonah had told him, that he'd cheated on Amber because she "couldn't do everything" in the bedroom.

He was looking at Silence. Waiting. Hopefully.

Silence wanted to break his nose.

Abhorrent piece of shit.

Silence had no qualms about leaving him hanging.

He pointed to the steering wheel. "Drive."

Jonah exhaled. He squared up to the wheel again, lowered the brake, put the stick into first, and they took off.

CHAPTER SIX

A REALIZATION CAME TO JONAH, and it almost made him laugh out loud: the stink of filthy people reminded him of Amber.

There was a long line of homeless individuals outside the Morrison Mission—a drab, two-story brick building, a repurposed factory—and their combined sour stench was overpowering, a reaction that almost made Jonah feel guilty. Handwritten signs on neon green tagboard proclaimed today to be the mission's celebrated "Meals on Monday." The local homeless were not missing out on the opportunity.

This was just the sort of thing that Amber would have been keen on. She got as excited about giving back as other people did about their weekly sitcoms. But the fact that these incredibly smelly people outside the Morrison Mission—who were almost entirely men—reminded Jonah of his sweet wife nearly made him chuckle. It would be the first time he'd laughed in weeks.

And since this charitable place was so perfectly Amber, he was growing more and more frustrated that Brett insisted on investigating it. What was the point of investigating something so obvious?

Jonah followed behind Brett's tall frame to his latest quarry, a white guy in a brown field jacket and a blue toboggan hat with a red pompom and large tear in the side.

"Weasel. You know him?" Brett said.

The man shook his head, the pompom flopping from side to side. He gave Brett a wary look.

Brett moved forward, continuing their path next to the line of people shuffling into the mission. Jonah followed. This had been Brett's technique: ask that abrupt question with his intense stare and stone-troll voice, receive a negative response, assume the question was heard by the nearby people in the line, move forward four places or so, and ask the next man. Repeat.

Jonah sighed.

Why, oh why had he done this? Whoever Brett was—charitable benefactor, private investigator hired by a charitable benefactor, OPD Internal Affairs officer, government investigator—this was stupid. Just stupid. And it was making Jonah think that Brett was nothing more than a crackpot.

"Weasel. You know him?"

A black man in a patchwork leather jacket and laceless hiking boots shook his head.

Brett moved on.

All right. Jonah had had enough. He hurried forward, catching up to Brett, tapped him on the back.

"Come on, man," Jonah said. "I told you, this is a dead end. This must be another one of Amber's volunteering things. Let's head to the press conference."

Brett ignored him, continued up the line.

"Weasel. You know—"

A voice from behind them. "I know him."

An old guy, not standing in line but leaning against a

lamppost. Stringy white hair dangling over a stringy face with a stringy beard. Tall. Jeans and an orange T-shirt, rotten with holes, bearing the logo and phone number of an out-of-state barbecue joint.

Brett stepped past Jonah, approached the man. Jonah followed.

"You're looking for Weasel, huh?"

Brett nodded.

"Haven't seen that guy in ten years. Shit, man, I ain't even heard the name."

Brett nodded again.

"Talk," he said, prompting the man, kindly almost. It was amazing how much inflection Brett could get out of his demon growl.

"What's to say? When I knew him, he wasn't nothing but a strung-out junkie. Heroin. You can see it in the eyes, man. Tiny little pupils. And track marks on the arm."

"Description," Brett said.

The man narrowed his eyes and grinned at Brett. "Man, what the *hell* is wrong with your voice?"

Brett just stared at him.

The man shrugged. "Black guy, pretty big. But, you know, losing mass 'cause of the poison. Sunken cheeks. Skittish as all hell. Nervous." He laughed. "Don't know where he came from. Just showed up one day. Hadn't never seen him around here before. They say..."

The man trailed off, scratched at his beard, narrowed his eyes at Brett, suddenly skeptical, as though a voice in his head had implored him to stop saying so much.

"They say what?" Brett said.

"You guys cops?"

Brett shook his head.

The man looked up and down the line of people, to the

far end of the street. Paranoia. "You know what, I ... I've said too much already."

He turned.

Brett reached out, caught him by his thin bicep, brought him to a halt.

"Talk."

The man took another glance at the surroundings, scratched his beard again, then looked from Jonah back to Brett. "They say he'd been a cop, kicked off the force."

Jonah's mind flashed on Amber's investigation and her position as a dispatcher, a job she'd held for only two years.

Weasel had been a cop.

A junkie cop from ten years prior.

A decade ago—when this man claimed to have last seen Weasel—Amber would have only been about fifteen. Not yet a dispatcher. Just a child.

The daughter of a different cop.

One in District C11.

Brett gave Jonah a look, then faced the man again.

"Weasel was a regular here for a year or so," the man continued. "Then, poof!, he was gone again. Ain't seen him since."

"Why remember him?" Brett said.

The man grinned. "Oh, it's hard to forget ol' Weasel. Because he didn't just like the skag. He liked women. Liked 'em a whole lot. Too much. Know what I mean?" He shook his head, gave an exhalation of combined disgust and morbid humor. "Those gals were never the same after they met the Weasel."

CHAPTER SEVEN

HE COULD SMELL the losers from a block away. Literally.

Finley had the Accord's windows sealed tight, engine running, a trickle of air-conditioning taking the edge off. But even in his protective bubble, even from his position parked on the opposite side of the road, a block away from the end of the line, the stink of the homeless queued up outside the Morrison Mission was apparent. Not constant, though. It hit him every few seconds, out of nowhere, pungent sneak attacks.

He was used to dealing with losers in his line of work, but those he encountered had *some* money, a place to live. They didn't exist in their own filth.

He angled the vents down. Might help a bit.

Why the hell was he here?

Scratch that.

He knew why he was here. He was here because Jonah Lund and the tall man were here.

But why were *they* here?

The mystery guy must have been another private investigator. The constant surveillance Finley's employer had put on

Lund had shown that he hadn't been in contact with his last investigator in weeks. It had seemed that Lund had given up on his search, even if he hadn't given up in the press. Why, then, had he suddenly hired a new investigator?

The first two PIs had been locals, easily recognizable to Finley. But this guy—Finley had never seen him before.

An hour ago, when Finley had arrived outside Lund's apartment, there had been a brief period before the two of them left and went to his Fiero. Finley had seen a tall man in dark clothes—a dark gray pair of slacks, black sport coat, light gray shirt beneath. Dark, choppy hair. Angular face. Someone completely unknown to Finley.

And when the Fiero took off, Finley assumed he knew where it was going. He was wrong. He'd followed at a safe distance through progressively deteriorating environs until they ended up at the Morrison Mission.

Lund and his investigator were at the right *kind* of place, but nowhere near where they actually needed to be.

Interesting.

But quite confusing.

Finley would continue to follow. No need to call the boss yet. Not until this made more sense.

Lund and his companion had walked down the line, questioning several of the slobs, finally landing a talker who'd been standing by a lamppost. The conversation concluded, and the bum walked off. Lund and the tall man went back to the Fiero, which was parked across the street, and got in. Brake lights. It moved.

Finley put the Accord into gear and followed.

CHAPTER EIGHT

SILENCE HAD THOUGHT they would be alone, but it turned out he wasn't the only one with the idea of watching the press conference from the top of the three-story parking garage. The city of Orlando was even more transfixed by the ongoing story of Amber Lund's disappearance than he'd thought.

A small crowd had gathered along the garage's north-side parapet, looking down upon the larger crowd at the Orlando Police Headquarters below—a semi-circle of maybe a hundred people, reporters and photographers in the front and citizens behind, who filled a plaza in front of the main tower. They were spread around a podium loaded with microphones.

Vehicles occupied all the spaces on the top floor of the garage, but the rubber parking blocks sat about a yard off the parapet, giving plenty of room for the crowd to form. Beside Silence, Jonah had covered his head with the hood of his Baja jacket, concealing as much of his face as possible. Under the hood, he'd also thrown on a baseball cap and a pair of Ray-Bans for good measure. His hands were in the jacket's front pocket-pouch, and he stole quick, furtive glances at the people on either side of them. So far, no one seemed to have recognized him.

The sun was already breaking through the gray cover that had recently formed, little streaks of bright blue here and there. A faint drizzle didn't so much fall from the sky but drifted down. Speeding traffic hissed by on Interstate 4, which was adjacent to the police complex and the parking garage, elevated on mammoth concrete columns.

The sprawling OPD complex comprised several massive buildings, stately yet plain, the cautiously planned beauty of twentieth-century bureaucracy. A tower rose above the other buildings, one that Jonah had said once served as a jail as well. You could see inmates looking down at you from the windows, he'd said. The landscaping that flowed through the complex was less self-conscious than the buildings, all bushes and flowers and palm trees and luscious green lawns.

A few uniformed cops kept the crowd at a distance from the podium, behind which were three men and a woman, all in business wear, several feet back.

One of the men approached the podium. Silence remembered him from the photos he'd seen that morning, before taking the private jet the Watchers had arranged for him to Orlando. Carlton Stokes. Earlier Silence had noted that Stokes looked like a cranky police lieutenant character from a TV show or a 1980s cop movie. Now, in flesh-and-blood, his features seemed softer, and he evoked a classic sitcom dad.

"That's Carlton," Jonah said, unaware of Silence's familiarity.

Behind Carlton, another man went to the microphone as well but stopped a few feet short, hands going behind his back, head lowered respectfully. He was a bit younger than Carlton, though his beard was mostly white. Aside from a slight gut, he was in good shape. Silence could sense the sadness in his eyes, his lowered face.

"Who's that?" Silence said, pointing.

Jonah stole another cautious look around them, inched closer to Silence. "Gavin Stokes. Carlton's brother, Amber's uncle. Moved away eight years ago. Lost touch with Amber, but not by choice."

Silence cocked his head.

"See, Carlton never liked Gavin's influence. Amber and Gavin had been close while she grew up, but Carlton thought he was a loser who was dragging Amber down. When Gavin moved to Texas for a teaching gig, Amber was about sixteen, seventeen, getting close to college age, leave-the-house-and-take-on-life age, so Carlton took the opportunity to tell his brother to stop contacting Amber."

Silence studied Gavin Stokes. The wind tussled his auburn hair, white at the temples. His face remained down-turned, wan with melancholy. He shifted in place, hands plunged into the pockets of a short pea jacket. Gavin Stokes didn't strike Silence as the bad influence type. More of a warm avuncular type, which was evidently exactly what he had been to Amber.

Silence felt eyes upon him. Turned.

A figure. By the parapet but standing back, far enough out of line with the other individuals that it caught Silence's attention. And as soon as he turned, the figure disappeared back into the crowd.

He thought of the Honda Accord.

Twenty minutes earlier when he and Jonah had crossed the parking lot of the luxury apartment complex, there had been a silver Accord, idling, at the back corner of the lot nestled among a few other cars as inconspicuously as possible. But idling vehicles always grabbed Silence's attention.

Especially when they end up tailing you.

The Accord had followed Jonah's Fiero here to the press conference. The driver had done a damn good job—hovering a suitable distance back, keeping several cars between them—but not good enough. Silence had monitored the Accord in the passenger mirror for the entire journey.

Below, Carlton Stokes spoke.

"Thank you all for joining us here today. As you know, this is an incredibly difficult time for the Stokes family."

His amplified voice boomed off the surrounding walls, off the gray columns holding I-4 in the air.

"My daughter, Amber, has been missing now for two months. Whatever was going through her head in that early morning on State Road 50, we can only guess. What I do know is that her car was found a couple miles from a bus station, tickets were purchased that evening in cash, and she had just married a man everyone felt was beneath her, a man who violated her trust. And it's this very man who's keeping the story in the press."

Silence sensed Jonah tense beside him. From his peripheral, he saw the younger man pull in tighter under his jacket.

"*That's* why my family is tormented at a time when we're already suffering enough."

Stokes's voice grew louder, cracking in an echo throughout the parking garage.

"That's why I've gathered you here for this press conference, here among the people who have been so good to the Stokes family for so many years."

With a broad swing of his arm, he gestured to the grand campus of buildings surrounding him, the power and venerability of the police department poured in concrete, chiseled from stone.

"What Mr. Lund implies is that the sordid past of District C11, the district I used to work for as a police officer, is somehow a factor in Amber's disappearance, that the enemies of the district have somehow taken their revenge, done something horrible to my daughter. Can you imagine? At a time like this, he's not only implying that something has happened to Amber, his *wife*, but also tarnishing my honorable service record."

He paused, and the microphones picked up his deep breath, slow release.

"My daughter is a bride who waited two weeks too long to run away from the altar. My daughter is alive. Amber, if you're listening ... if you're listening, sweetheart, there are people who love you. We don't know why you've stayed away so long. Everyone just wants to know you're safe. Come home to us."

Another pause.

"My daughter is alive. Thank you for your time."

Stokes stepped back, head lowering, hand going to his eyes. His brother went to him, put his arm around him. The lawyers, too, approached, and the group headed for the tower behind them. The reporters erupted with questions and camera flashes, but the uniformed officers kept them at a distance. The citizens dispersed, heading away from the headquarters, crossing the street.

At the doors of the tower, Gavin Stokes said a few final words to his brother, then turned and headed toward the garage, head lowered, hands in his pockets.

This could be an opportunity.

Silence got Jonah's attention, pointed over the parapet at Gavin. "We find him. You make introduction."

The crowd on the top floor parking garage, too, was disbanding, most funneling toward the bulkhead, some finding their vehicles.

And as Silence turned around, he saw the figure, just a shadowy silhouette in the bulkhead's doorway, looking in his direction before quickly turning and disappearing into the crowd.

———

On the first floor, people were getting into their cars, engines firing up, a line of traffic slowly snaking to the exit.

A few feet away was Gavin Stokes, getting into a dark green Jeep Grand Cherokee. Closer to him, Silence noted more details—thick hair on a mature hairline, very much full of its youthful color—medium brown, almost reddish—until about halfway down his head, at which point it rapidly whitened, especially in the sideburns where it met with the white of his beard.

Jonah called out to him. "Gavin!"

Gavin stopped, looked, keys in hand. His mouth opened when he spotted Jonah.

"What are you doing here?" he hissed, looking at the people around them getting into their cars as Silence and Jonah stopped beside him.

Jonah motioned toward Silence. "My, um ... associate, Brett, here is helping me."

Gavin looked at Silence with his sad eyes.

"Nice to meet ya," he said halfheartedly.

Silence nodded. "Pleasure."

Gavin gave the standard shocked reaction to Silence's grotesque voice, followed by the standard attempt at covering up his rudeness. He cleared his throat. "Are you a private dick?"

"Of a sort."

Usually he would have answered that question with a shake of the head. This time, though, ambiguity seemed fitting of the situation.

"Me too," Gavin said. "Part-time, anyway."

"Weasel. You know him?"

Silence heard Jonah sigh.

Gavin cocked his head. "Beg your pardon?"

Silence took his PenPal notebook from his pocket. PenPals' plastic covers came in a variety of bold colors. This one was red. He flipped it open, removed Amber's sticky note, and handed the note to Gavin, who gave it a puzzled twist of the lips.

"What is this?"

"It's Amber's," Silence said.

Now that he realized what he was holding, Gavin held the note like a fragile artifact, a religious relic. His mouth fell open. "Where did you get it?"

"Our apartment," Jonah said. "Cops overlooked it."

Gavin nodded slowly, staring at the note. "Yeah, I know the Weasel."

An endorphin rush of potential fluttered through Silence.

Gavin finally looked up from the note, to Jonah. "Ray Beasley."

Jonah's eyes widened.

Gavin turned to Silence. "He was a cop, in C11 with Carlton. Got kicked off the force for heroin use. But before that, when Amber was a kid, he was a big part of her life. A surrogate uncle. She called me and Ray her 'two uncles.'" He paused. "And then she lost both of us. Within a few years of each other. Ray went nuts with drugs, and Carlton excommunicated me from her life."

He looked back through the open side of the parking garage toward the headquarters complex. Silence let him be, allowed the moment to breathe.

Gavin turned back around, and Silence held out his hand for the sticky note.

Jonah stepped toward Gavin, took the VHS tape from the front pocket of his jacket, handed it to him.

Gavin looked it over, raised an eyebrow.

"A video for me. From Amber," Jonah said. "I ... can't watch it. Hold on to it for me?"

Gavin nodded, looked deep into Jonah, his jaw set. "You think her disappearance is related to C11, don't you? Some shit my brother got involved in, someone he pissed off getting revenge, taking it out on his daughter."

"You know I do."

They looked at each other.

Gavin set his jaw. "And you think she's dead. I can see it in your eyes."

A pause from Jonah.

"Yes, I do."

Gavin looked from Jonah to Silence, back to Jonah.

"She's alive."

He stepped back to the Grand Cherokee, climbed inside, and slammed the door.

CHAPTER NINE

JONAH FOLLOWED Brett up the stairs, back to the third floor where they'd grabbed one of the last remaining spots to park his Fiero.

When they'd first arrived, Jonah had noted that the parking garage was on the nicer side. Not a big, squarish, gray thing like so many of them. This one had rounded corners, contrasting brick and concrete, green accents—a dark, bluish, copper-patina type of green.

The builders hadn't skimped on the stairwell. Its outfacing side was covered in similar green glass, giving the outside views a surreal quality. The concrete was smooth and clean. And there were trash cans and large concrete planters with a few spiky plants at the ground floor and on each landing.

By the time they'd finished the conversation with Gavin, the crowd had disappeared, and so they were the only ones in the stairwell, their footsteps echoing.

She's alive, Gavin had said.

He'd been so demonstrative. Such fire in his eyes. But he

hadn't been certain. His words had come out with the ferocity of deep determination, sadly biased denial.

Jonah was being more pragmatic. As much of a goof-off as people thought him to be, he still knew that when push came to shove, logic, not emotion, was what got a person through life. And logic told him that Amber was dead. Jonah's preemptive grieving had been an act of pragmatism.

And yet, every time he heard someone like Gavin say, with such passion, such clarity, that Amber was alive, something sparked inside Jonah.

Maybe...

One thing was certain of, however, was that Amber hadn't run off to "find herself," as Carlton and so many others had said. She and Jonah had made great strides with Dr. Nogulich, and by the time they left, handing each other the VHS tapes, Jonah knew things were going to be all right. He'd seen it. In her perfect blue eyes. He *knew*.

Amber wasn't the most intelligent of individuals—as her father was always so quick to point out—but she was very wise and more than self-aware enough to realize her naïveté made her an easy target in the harsh wide world. No, she wasn't out there somewhere off the grid. She wasn't living in a tent in the middle of a national park. She hadn't skipped the country to sip ayahuasca and meditate with a shaman somewhere in South America.

Something had happened to her.

District Cii.

An old grudge. A gang leader who hadn't received a promised favor twenty years ago. A recently released ex-con who felt he should have been slid under the table like so many others.

Amber was gone because of something connected to those bastards. Jonah was certain of it.

It must have been this certainty that had led Jonah here,

to this stairwell, following this tall man with the Frankenstein voice who refused to give his proper name.

Jonah watched the man as he ascended the stairs. The small muscles in the back of Brett's neck twitched with his steps. It wasn't a massive neck, nothing about him screamed bodybuilder, but everything was just ... *strong*. His power exuded from him, and he tamed it with a layer of classy-chic clothing.

Brett looked back, over his shoulder, not making eye contact with Jonah, rather looking behind them, down the steps. He'd been like this all morning—always a watchful eye, careful monitoring of his surroundings.

They reached the landing between the second and third floors, pivoted. And as they continued up to the final landing, Brett slowed slightly, looked over his shoulder again, eyes squinted, as though listening.

At the third-floor landing, he quickly, silently pulled to the side, along the edge of the wall. He held a finger to his mouth in a shushing motion, and swiped his other hand to the side, telling Jonah to join him.

"What—"

Brett clamped his hand over Jonah's mouth hard. Damn hard. His thick, rough fingers pressed Jonah's lips into his teeth, nearly making his eyes water.

As quietly as he could with his gravelly voice, Brett whispered, "Being followed."

He pointed at the stairs.

Jonah's forehead was instantly cool, wet—panic sweat.

His mind flashed on District C11 again.

All the trouble the district was involved in, all the inconclusive investigations. Informants murdered by gangland toughs. Missing persons.

Goddamn bastards.

And now someone was following him and Brett...

Footsteps.

Quiet, slow, deliberate footsteps coming from the stairs, pausing occasionally, as though the person was stopping to listen. Each footstep louder, drawing nearer.

Jonah's imagination flittered. Some drug lord who had a vendetta against Carlton. Or a cheap but efficient hitman. Someone involved with Amber's disappearance.

The footsteps continued. Almost to the landing. Right around the corner.

Then a figure appeared. Dressed fully in black. Pants, shirt, beanie. Jonah saw the man for only a moment, got just the vaguest view of the man's shape, his short height, small size—before Brett grabbed him.

A flash, a rustle of clothing, and the man was in the air, lifted off his feet by the throat. Brett slammed him into the concrete wall.

BOOM!

Brett got into the man's face, an inch away.

"Talk!"

Thrashing limbs. Hands clawing at Brett's forearms. Feet flailing six inches off the floor. Gurgles from the man's throat.

Brett pulled the man away from the wall and slammed him back into it.

BOOM!

The impact shook the walls, its sound screaming down the stairwell.

"Talk!"

Louder gurgling from the man's throat.

Commotion from the garage beyond, on the other side of the steel door. An additional set of footsteps. Someone was approaching.

With one hand pinning the man against the wall, Brett reached out and grabbed the concrete planter that sat in the corner, fingers plunging into the soil, dragged it across the floor—the crunch of concrete against concrete—and brought it to rest against the metal door with a *clang*, another sound that boomed up and down the stairwell.

Shit, that thing must have weighed a hundred pounds, and he'd moved it like it was aluminum.

Brett straightened back up, face to face with the flailing, pinned man.

It was then that Jonah got his first good glimpse of the other guy.

And saw curly dark hair poking from the bottom of the hat. Pale, soft skin. Slender arms and hands.

It wasn't a guy at all. It was a young woman.

And Jonah recognized her.

"*Wait!!*" He grabbed Brett's forearm. "Wait, I know her!"

Brett's snarling face turned to him, slackened.

"Put her down!"

Someone on the other side of the door tried to enter. The door clanked into the planter.

Brett brought the woman to her feet, took his hand from her throat.

It was Kim Hurley, Amber's friend, someone Jonah had known for years.

She bent over, hands on her knees, coughing.

Tapping at the door. The touch bar rattled violently. A man's voice. "What's going on in there?"

Kim coughed louder, hacking. Quivering hands cupped her knees. Drool fell from her mouth, puddled between her black, chunky-heeled boots.

"You could have killed her!" Jonah said.

Brett looked at him. "Who is?"

"Kim Hurley. Amber's best friend. She's clean, man. She was our maid of honor two months ago, for God's sake."

Kim straightened up, gasping but no longer coughing. She rubbed her throat.

Brett approached her. "Why following?"

"I'm ... I'm not. Well, I mean, I am, but..."

She stopped. Grimaced. A sudden wave of pain. She rubbed her throat harder.

The tapping on the door grew louder, changed to pounding. "What the *hell* is going on in there?"

Brett growled, swooped across the landing, yanked the planter aside, and threw open the door. "Go *away*."

A thin man in glasses and a green flannel did exactly as Brett commanded, scurrying off into the garage.

Brett slid the planter back into place, looked at Kim.

"I've been keeping tabs on Jonah," she said, a finger pointed at him, "since he's the one keeping Amber's story alive. I just ... want to know, want to believe she's still alive."

"Bullshit," Brett snarled. He swallowed. "You're on a team."

"A ... a team?"

Brett pointed through the green glass. "Accord. Who's your friend?"

Jonah looked to where Brett was pointing. Across the street, a silver Honda Accord was parked beneath the I-4 overpass. A silhouette behind the driver's seat was just visible.

Kim shook her head. "What??"

Brett got closer to her. He didn't say "Talk" again, just stared into her, hard, enough to make her tremble, cower away, look out the window at the car.

"I'm telling you, I don't know who that is, and ... *there!* There's a cop right there. I'll scream. He'll see me with Jonah."

Jonah looked over her shoulder. Outside, between the headquarters and the interstate, was a squad car with blue lights flashing, an officer standing beside it, a lingering crowd control officer.

"She's right," he said to Brett. "Please. Let her be. She's Amber's friend, man!"

Brett glared at him, then at her. Then he stepped back, giving her space.

She looked at Jonah, eyes wet, chest heaving.

"Kim..." Jonah said.

Her hands shook, fluttered. Her eyes darted between Jonah and Brett.

And then she pivoted, sprinted down the stairs, her palm screeching on the handrail, the thunder of her footsteps echoing harshly.

"Kim, wait!" Jonah called after her.

He turned to Brett.

Who was already dragging the planter back into place.

Brett pulled the door open and exited into the garage.

CHAPTER TEN

IN THE SHADE beneath the overpass, Finley looked through a pair of 10x25 binoculars, through the Accord's windshield, to the top panel of dark green glass of the stairwell that ran up the center of the three-story garage.

Though the glass was tinted, it was perfectly clear, and Finley had seen everything that had happened, the full confrontation, in shades of emerald, a bit of drama playing out in a wine bottle. For a while there, it looked like the guy was going to kill her, snuff her out right there against the stairwell wall, but after he'd released her and there had been a few moments of conversation, he'd let the woman go.

"Kim, you dumb bitch," Finley uttered, his binoculars tracing her movement as she turned around the final mid-level landing and headed for the ground floor.

Why the *shit* was Kim Hurley here? And why was she talking to Jonah Lund and his mystery companion, this large and evidently violent man?

Finley would need to contact his employer about these developments. He couldn't put it off any longer.

But more pressing was the fact that it had appeared as

though the big guy had, during his conversation with Kim, pointed out the window *at Finley*, at the Accord which Finley had parked covertly, expertly among other vehicles.

Surely not...

Surely Finley hadn't been spotted. After all, Finley was good. The best. He wouldn't be found out.

Finley's exacting perfection was one of necessity. He wouldn't jeopardize this job, this opportunity, this second chance. He had a new life, a great life, and it would not be taken from him.

Kim reached the bottom of the stairwell and exited. She gave a furtive glance to her surroundings and hurried down the road.

Finley brought the binoculars back up, looking to the top of the garage, where he could just see the roof of the Fiero over the parapet. Lund and the big man stood by the car, talking. A few last words, and they separated, Lund getting into the driver's side and the big man walking around the backside of the vehicle.

The man opened the passenger door. And stopped. Looked over the edge of the roof. Right at Finley.

Shit.

Yes, Finley had been discovered.

This guy was good, whoever he was. Finley was going to have to up his game.

But first he had to get the hell out of there.

He put the Accord into gear and pulled away.

CHAPTER ELEVEN

A ROW OF STATELY, brand-new townhouses. Their proximity to the quiet street in front varied, giving them a staggered appearance. Their designs, too, were varied—some with front porches, some without; some with a single dormer window, some with two—as were the colors, types, and materials of their siding. Their cute charm gave a bit of a New England seaside vibe while their stacked, row-house layout gave hints of Brooklyn, right in the middle of Florida. The landscaping was brand new—saplings held by support wires, mounds of pine straw mulch, palm trees with freshly pruned fronds.

Across the street was an equally new shopping area with pleasant, clean, upscale establishments—a coffee shop, two restaurants, a toy store. A small crowd was gathered around the monitors at an outdoor seating area.

It wasn't the sort of neighborhood where Silence would have expected to find a heroin addict.

He and Jonah took a sidewalk to the front porch of the brightest of the townhouses on the block—the siding on the bottom floor was yellow and that on the top floor was wood shingles.

Jonah huffed again. The third time he'd done so since they exited the Fiero. His hands were clenched, fingers pulsing. Silence took his shoulder, stopped him in his tracks, looked at him. They'd spent enough time together already that Jonah was picking up on his non-verbal clues, and with this one, Silence said, *You okay?*

Jonah took a deep breath, looked at the townhouse then to Silence. "Back at the mission. The guy said that Beasley hurts women. This guy helped raise her ... when she was a little, vulnerable girl." He gave Silence a dark, prompting look. "And I found his name by her phone the night she disappeared."

"Hearsay," Silence said.

"I know it's hearsay, but..." He trailed off, took another long look at the townhouse. "Let's go."

He took off. Silence followed.

The doorbell had a shiny brass casing, and when Silence pushed the button, there was a pleasant series of melodic rings from within the house, muffled by the walls and door. Footsteps. And a man opened the door, only a few inches.

Black, fifties, white hair. Thick forearms on a mostly in-shape physique. Big face, full cheeks, a bit of a second chin. Polo shirt, khakis.

Aside from the height, he didn't match the description given at the homeless mission, and aside from the telltale bloodshot eyes, he looked about as much like a heroin addict as his neighborhood looked like that of a heroin addict.

The man squinted at them. "Yes?"

"Ray Beasley?" Silence said.

A pause. Beasley's reaction skipped right over the standard surprise at Silence's growly voice and went into instant panic, eyes going wide. "How did you find me?"

"I know people."

Ray Beasley had been unlisted in the Orlando phone

book, but a quick call to a Specialist had resolved the issue. In the process, Silence had learned that Beasley had changed his name years earlier.

Silence didn't understand all the Watchers' methods—indeed, he was meant not to—but he knew members were embedded in all levels of government. Given their technicians, called Specialists, had access to the highest levels of classified intelligence, basic biographical information was small potatoes—things like current and past addresses, birth and death certificates, death records, and name changes.

Beasley looked to Jonah, standing just behind Silence. "You're Amber's husband. What is this?"

Jonah stepped closer to the door. "We just want to talk to you."

Beasley's arm quivered. His hand went around the corner of the doorframe. His shoulder dropped slightly. Going for something.

Silence bashed into the door. Beasley backpedaled, shoes squeaking on the tile of the entryway. Silence's hand wrapped around the barrel of the shotgun. Cold metal on his fingers.

He took advantage of Beasley's momentum, using the weapon clenched between them as a yoke, swinging him to the side and into a wall, hard. Nearby picture frames rattled. He jerked the gun to the side, freed it, and shoved the barrel laterally into Beasley's throat. The man gagged.

Jonah was behind him.

"Shut door," Silence said without taking his eyes off Beasley.

The squeal of hinges and the *thunk* of the door closing.

He lessened the pressure on the shotgun.

Beasley sucked in a breath. "How the hell did you find me? I told you years ago, I wouldn't say anything else. That I was done with it all. You're here because of Amber, aren't you? I know nothing. I ... I..."

Jonah approached. "You think we're connected to Cɪɪ."

"Aren't you?"

"No," Silence said. He lowered the shotgun a bit more, then pulled out his PenPal, flipped it open to Amber's note, held it in front of Beasley's face. "Talk."

Beasley squinted. "That's the address of the Morrison Mission. Who wrote this?"

"Amber. Explain."

"I ... I have no idea."

Jonah stepped beside Silence, rested a hand on the shotgun's stock. "Can we put this away?" His tone was mediating, soft.

Silence considered it. He lowered the gun, broke it open, popped the shells out, dropped them in his pocket, then put the gun back by the door frame.

"The note was by her phone," Jonah said. "The night she disappeared."

"I haven't talked to Amber in ... God, it must be six or seven years. Not since, you know, I got kicked out. Heroin."

Silence held the note up again, right in Beasley's face, an inch away, tapped where Amber had written his pseudonym.

"Weasel," Silence said.

"That's what they called me, yeah. I was a junkie. And a rat."

"And an abuser."

"Huh?"

"Of women."

Beasley's shoulders dropped. "Yeah, man. I did. Hookers, you know? I used to slap them around a little." He paused. "No. No, it was more than that. I beat the shit out of 'em. Sent a few to the hospital. Nearly killed one. I was a monster. A real weasel. But people can change. Look around you, man. I've cleaned myself up. Done good for the world. Started a business. Volunteer work."

Silence pointed at his eyes. "But still taking."

Beasley cocked his head.

"Bloodshot," Silence said.

"Oh." Beasley scoffed, shook his head. "I'm not taking, asshole. I'll show you why my eyes are bloodshot."

He shifted past Silence and Jonah, back to the front door, which he swung open hard enough that it *cracked* into the wall. He pointed. "Go see for yourself."

Silence stepped over, looked outside to where he was pointing—the sports bar across the street, the one with a crowd formed around the television sets outside.

"Amber called me her uncle," Beasley said. "But to me she wasn't a niece. She was more like a daughter. Remember that."

His bloodshot eyes filled with tears. One escaped, raced down his cheek. He swiped it away.

Silence looked at him. Then stepped past, back into the sunshine. Jonah followed. The door slammed shut behind them. A deadbolt thudded into place.

Silence put his hands in his pockets as he walked down the sidewalk. His mind mulled over everything he'd just heard.

It was a quiet street, pristinely landscaped. Silence and Jonah strolled across it to the sports bar, stepped to the back of the crowd. There were no cheers, no drunken exclamations from the onlookers. Rather there were whispers, shudders, Oh-my-Gods.

A projector screen television filled the wall behind the bar. Wall-mounted television sets were scattered throughout the space. All the screens showed local news programs. The screen closest to Silence bore a large headline:

AMBER LUND'S BODY DISCOVERED

CHAPTER TWELVE

Silence slowly turned his head, looking out the corner of his eye. Beside him, Jonah wore the same non-expressive look as when they first met. That blank, not quite emotional, not quite upset expression.

Silence stepped away from Jonah, toward one of the television sets that bore closed captioning. He didn't want to encourage Jonah to join him, uncertain of the younger man's emotional state. But Jonah followed.

A gray strip of empty highway crossed the bottom of the screen, and beyond, a flat marshland dotted with palms and pine trees stretched to the horizon. An ambulance was to the left, cop cars on the right, all the vehicles' lights flashing. The energy was languid and careful as a group of uniformed personnel lifted a stretcher, covered with a white blanket, over the guardrail.

The close captioning read:

AND EARLY REPORTS INDICATE THE BODY WAS FOUND ON STATE ROAD 50 OUTSIDE TITUSVILLE,

IN A PATCH OF BRUSH, HALF-SUBMERGED. A
PASSING MOTORIST MADE THE SIGHTING.

"They checked that area. Impossible," Jonah said.
Although his face was still emotionless, there was pain and
disgust in his tone.

SOURCES INFORM CHANNEL 16 THAT DRUGS
HAVE BEEN DETECTED IN LUND'S SYSTEM. A SAD
DAY IN THIS EVER-EVOLVING STORY, BUT AT
LEAST NOW LUND'S FAMILY AND FRIENDS HAVE
SOME MODICUM OF CLOSURE. STAN.

The camera went from a pretty, middle-aged blonde
woman to a suited and dignified, silver-haired gentleman of
maybe sixty. Stan. In the graphical rectangle over his shoulder
was an image related to a new story—a baby panda bear. Stan
spoke. Closed captioning said that the zoo had welcomed a
recent addition.

Silence turned to Jonah. He was the same. That same
look. Even with the bit of reaction in his tone moments
earlier, nothing had changed about his face. And as Silence
considered this, trying to make sense of it, Jonah suddenly
turned and rushed off.

He went to the wrought iron, decorative trashcan a few
feet behind them. And vomited.

Someone laughed.

Silence approached him.

Jonah's hands were on the flared lip of the trashcan recep-
tacle, his fingers wrapped around it tightly, interlaced in the
gaps, head hung over the gaping hole in the center, drool
dripping down, coughing.

An image flashed through Silence's mind.

An image of himself. In his previous life. With his previous face and previous voice and previous name. Before the incident, the surgery, his conscription into the Watchers. A disembodied view. A floating camera. The man who Silence had been, crouched on a mansion's hardwood floor, in a pool of blood.

C.C.'s body.

She was face down.

Cold.

Black hair splayed in the blood.

A hole in the back of her head.

The man who would become Silence had heaved. Like Jonah just had.

And then the man who would become Silence had passed out.

Jonah wiped his mouth with the back of his hand. Straightened up. Put one hand to his stomach.

A wave of empathy flushed over Silence, a peculiar feeling of connection. Something from his old self fired off in the back of his mind, flickers of what he had been, the compassion. He wanted to reach out to Jonah, embrace him.

But he didn't.

Silence remembered the judgement he had leveled at Jonah, not an hour ago, when he found out why the man had cheated on his then-fiancée, when he found out that it had been only a matter of months ago.

"Abhorrent piece of shit" was the snap-judgment title his mind had conjured for Jonah.

Which seemed trite now. And petty.

"Go home," Silence said as quietly, as gently as he could.

Jonah took a deep breath, cleaned his lips again, looked at the back of his hand and wiped it on his jeans quickly, embarrassed.

He shook his head.

"Go home," Silence said again. He swallowed. "Meet tomorrow."

"No. Let's continue. Come on."

And before Silence could respond, Jonah stepped away.

CHAPTER THIRTEEN

GAVIN STOKES WAS in complete darkness.

A tumult of deep reds and shadowy grays swam before his closed eyes. His body swam too, violent twists of his torso, swings of his arms, tossing the abstract distortions, twirling and skewing them.

The sight of Amber's body on the newscast. The confirmation of her death coming from a television set. Knowing that somehow she had met her end in the middle of a swamp. He pictured her beautiful, guiltless face in the murk, blonde hair stained brown and foul green.

Another round of tears coursed out of him, head between his knees, hands in his hair.

A thick scent. Flowery sweet. Lilac. Lingering notes of detergent or fabric softener, whatever had been used to clean the blanket that his face was buried in, a fleece throw that had been draped over the arm of the sofa.

The smell of lilac would be associated with his niece's death, every time he smelled it, from here on out. Forever. He could predict that bit of the future.

A wave of anger. He pulled at his hair hard enough to water his eyes more.

This was an injustice. He didn't know what had happened to her. But it was an *injustice*.

He could already hear the cynical voice of the collective in his head, the increasingly over-informed, opinionated public, saying that the drugs in Amber's system spoke to her character. They would say that drugs explained why Amber's car had veered off the road, gotten stuck in the mud.

But those voices, those people didn't know Amber. Gavin had been foolish, *stupid*, to have allowed himself to be separated from her in recent years, but he was never disconnected from her essence. Amber was pure. Whatever led her to drugs, it was not her fault.

None of this was her fault.

He knew it.

Why had she been taking drugs? *Why?*

Another surge of pain, so strong he felt it in his head, a tension in his skull, his brain. He was lightheaded for a moment. His fingers tingled. A dappling of sweat on his forehead, absorbed by the fleece blanket.

A realization. He'd heard nothing from the other side of the room for some time now. Minutes. He took his head from the blanket, opened his eyes.

Carlton was in the recliner opposite the sectional on which Gavin was sitting. It was his house, Carlton's, only seven years old, stylish yet not overbearing, trendy furniture and all the latest amenities. A bank of picture windows behind them, through which inappropriately chipper sunlight entered the room from the countryside beyond, blazing green and blue.

Carlton stared off. Motionless. Bloodshot, wet eyes. A tumbler of bourbon in his hand.

Gavin tried to speak. Couldn't.

He tried to stand. Couldn't.

Then he reminded himself again whose daughter Amber was.

Was.

He found his strength and stood, then stepped to his brother, placed a hand on his shoulder. "Carlton?"

Nothing. Motionless.

Gavin remained there for several long moments, keeping his hand on Carlton's shoulder almost as much to steady himself as to comfort his brother. The refrigerator hummed in the kitchen a few feet away. Additional humming from the ceiling vents, air conditioning that felt too cold.

Finally, Carlton spoke, that deep voice of his more gravelly than normal, not as loud. "Here," he said. He stood, wobbled, and trudged to the kitchen. He pulled open a drawer, retrieved a small paperback, and slowly made his way back to the recliner.

Gavin watched the book as he approached. He knew immediately what it was, from just a glimpse of the bright blue cover, the thin spine, a splash of red lettering in a distinctive font on the front cover.

Gavin's hands shook.

"Here," Carlton said again. "This was on her desk. One of the books you read to her, right?"

Gavin had to reach both hands out to take it. "Yes."

The Secret of Summerford Point
Kara, Kid Detective, Book 7

All of its edges—the outline of the cover, the text block, the corners—had been worn to a fuzzy, cloth-like texture through hours of gentle use.

Gavin's fingers trembled as he pulled back the front cover.

The pages within had yellowed with time, turning to a dark amber color.

Amber.

The comfortable scent of a used bookstore wafted from the pages. The copyright page showed a publication year of 1972.

In the upper right-hand corner of the first page, a blank page, was Amber's name in big, awkward, print letters, the handwriting of a second grader—*AMBER STOKES*.

And farther down the page, centered, were a few lines in an adult's handwriting. His handwriting. Gavin's.

Amber,

It has been a pleasure experiencing these wonderful mysteries with you. You are a real sleuth in the making.

Love,
Uncle Gavin

When Amber was a tiny girl, it had stunned Gavin to discover that Carlton didn't read to her, given that the two of them—he and Carlton—had read together as boys, voraciously. They devoured copious detective stories, long nights with flashlights and graham crackers and giggles. The habit led to a brotherly oath: they'd both grow up to become real-life detectives. The oath was honored, but Carlton was quick to point out that he'd become a real police detective, and Gavin was just a part-time private eye.

Since Amber's mother had died when she was young and Carlton wasn't reading to her, Gavin filled the void, a great chance for him to bond with his niece and a way to perpetuate one of the warmest memories of his childhood—reading detective stories with a loved one. For years, until Amber finally grew too old, too cool, he read her scores of children's detective books. Her favorites were *Nancy Drew* and *Kara, Kid Detective*.

Reading to Amber was one of Gavin's most treasured memories, and apparently it was one of Amber's too. Because she'd held on to at least one of the books. For all these years.

Gavin held it in his hands.

He stepped back to the sectional, clutching the tiny book. The cover was slightly sticky, a child's possession, read at night with a flashlight while eating surreptitious candy that sullied the fingers, sullied the cover.

He stared at it now, sitting between his knees, held between both his hands.

It had hit him like a punch seeing both of their handwritings within the front cover, his and that of a childhood version of Amber. And he didn't know if he could take another blow.

But he also clearly remembered how much Amber used to write in her books. Little notes. Underlinings. Highlights. Gavin had never been a fan of marking up a book, something he viewed as destructive and potentially changing the author's original intent. But he had never discouraged Amber, a young, plucky, would-be gumshoe. So he knew that if he turned the pages, he would see more evidence of young Amber in the form of her notes.

He wanted to.

But he didn't know if he had the strength.

He opened it anyway.

And there they were, just as he remembered. Amber's little musings.

What does this mean?

What is a buoy?

I like this!! So funny

He continued turning, saw his own name.

Uncle Gavin says I should look this up

He turned the page.

Kara is so COOL!!!

He flipped another page.
And stopped.
Something peculiar.
There was another one of her excited notes...

Oh no!! Kara is in trouble!

...and beneath it was a line of adult handwriting.

But this time the adult handwriting wasn't his own.

He recognized it from the sticky note Jonah and his associate, Brett, had shown him earlier in the day.

It was *Amber's* adult handwriting...

And the message was alarming.

I think I might be in trouble.

CHAPTER FOURTEEN

A PERKY, chipper little coffee shop/Internet café wasn't the sort of destination that Jonah would have expected from Brett, this tall, unsmiling, violent, mysterious man who Jonah was beginning to think was some sort of spy or assassin rather than a private detective.

The place was a bit bigger than Jonah's own coffee shop, seating maybe thirty people, which made sense given its dual purpose as an Internet café. He admired what they'd done with the place, a contrast to Roast and Relax, to which Jonah and his business partner had given a retro vibe. The aesthetic of this place fell somewhere between a Starbucks and the romanticized, deceivingly perfect coffee shops in primetime sitcoms. Quirky paintings, shelves with knickknacks, and a random guitar adorned the walls, one of which was olive green, the others light tan. Copper ceiling. Wooden, two-seat tables. Everything had a glowing, golden, earthy feel, except for one contrasting table, bright blue with white chairs. Along the far wall were several computer stations, Brett and Jonah's purpose for entering.

They soon found themselves at one of the seven matching

Macintosh computers. Jonah took a sip of his latte and watched as Brett hunched over the computer, squinting at the monitor. Beside him on the wooden counter was a steaming mug of regular coffee, black. Jonah would have thought that Brett would look out of place here, but his chic clothes and, surprisingly enough, his demeanor fit right in.

It's funny how places seem to adapt to people.

Jonah pulled his stool closer to Brett's, looked at the screen.

Brett had a program open, Netscape browser, a portal to the World Wide Web. The website that he'd accessed was Yahoo! search engine.

Brett dragged the mouse, bringing the cursor into the search field, clicked, then started typing. He used both hands, all fingers, in proper typing form, not pecking with two fingers as Jonah had noticed so many people over thirty doing. In the search field appeared:

"ray beasley" orlando

Again Jonah was impressed. Brett had Internet search savvy; he knew that placing search terms within quotation marks joined the contained words into one term, a better way of getting relevant, precise results.

A list appeared on the screen—hyperlinks with descriptions—and among them was an old police article from the archives of the *Orlando Defender*.

Police Apprehend Four in Late-Night Raid

Brett clicked the link, which brought up the *Defender's* website. The article was from 1986. Jonah leaned forward, trying to get a better look at the screen, but before he could, Brett was already dragging the scroll bar on the side of the screen, the text flying by, getting a rapid-fire assessment of the article.

A moment later, Brett brought the cursor to the top of the screen, highlighted the URL. But instead of typing a new URL, he began entering a long streak of numbers. His fingers moved rapidly, no hesitation, which meant he had this long number committed to memory. Jonah stopped counting after twenty digits.

"What's that you're entering? It's not a URL."

Brett didn't respond.

"Do you have this number *memorized?*"

Brett didn't respond.

Jonah's mind flashed to his thoughts moments earlier, those of Brett being something quite more than a private detective. He thought of the card Brett had handed him at their introduction. It had said he belonged to an "organization." No further clarification. Just an "organization."

Who was this guy?

And what the hell had Jonah gotten himself involved in? This secretive organization that—if it even existed—claimed to have a mission of helping people in need.

People like Jonah.

Which brought about another thought, one Jonah had been trying to deny.

The cause for his need.

Amber was dead.

He'd already processed the grief. A little less than two months ago. Not long after she disappeared. He'd known she was gone; he'd felt it in his bones.

And yet...

He refocused on the screen.

When Brett finished entering the long number and pressed *return*, a strange website appeared. In fact, it looked more like a piece of software than a website. Like the back end of a bank's computer network.

Or a governmental system of some sort...

Just a black screen with a pixelated, green cursor at the top, blinking.

Brett typed what he'd typed before, what he'd entered into Yahoo!, which appeared on the screen in green block text.

"ray beasley" orlando

A line of text immediately appeared below.

SCNND RSLTS — SPCLST APPRVL

Strange. And oddly technical looking, esoteric. Jonah's lips parted. He turned to look at Brett.

"What is this, Brett?"

He stared at the side of Brett's face—which was squinting, as though dissatisfied with the computer's results—and waited for a response.

Didn't receive one.

Brett drummed his fingers.

The growl of an espresso machine, quiet conversations and laughter.

A new question.

"Who are you?" Jonah said.

Again, no reply from Brett.

Brett was just about to type again when there was a shrill, electronic *BEEP*.

Jonah jumped.

The sound hadn't come from the computer. Brett pulled a pager from his pocket, looked at the small screen.

"Excuse me," he said.

He rose, leaned in front of Jonah, blocking his view of the computer monitor, and pressed *command–Q* on the keyboard, closing Netscape. The computer's desktop image showed again, a flat, turquoise field with small tilde shapes and an icon in the upper righthand corner that said *Macintosh HD*.

The mystery program was gone.

CHAPTER FIFTEEN

SILENCE STEPPED OUTSIDE to the sounds of plodding traffic on the four-lane street in front of him.

The coffee shop was in a ubiquitous area of commercial urban sprawl, all the brand names and recognizable logos that one could imagine lined up and down a street that was technically a highway but in town was constricted by numerous traffic lights. Strip mall after strip mall. Fast-food joint after fast-food joint. Utility lines dangling from an endless procession of wooden poles.

And someone watching him from a bench in front of a jewelry store, hidden mostly, but not entirely, by the trunk of a crape myrtle.

Mr. Honda Accord, no doubt.

Silence hadn't seen the man at Beasley's townhouse, but if he'd followed Silence here, that meant he had to have trailed him to Beasley's as well.

The guy was good.

C.C. had taught Silence how to tame his wayward thoughts, so he knew how to stay focused on one task while not forgetting about the others on his list.

He made a mental note of Mr. Accord's position and continued with the task at hand.

His beeper still in his left hand, he retrieved his cell phone with the other. The number on the beeper's tiny, brown LCD screen bore an 865 area code.

East Tennessee.

Lola.

Or, more likely, Mrs. Enfield calling via Lola's cellular phone, as Mrs. Enfield didn't have a cell of her own.

A single ring, and his call was answered.

"Si!" It was Mrs. Enfield. One syllable. That's all it took for him to tell she was in hysterics. "They took him! Surgery. They're cutting him up! My Baxter."

"I'm sorry." He swallowed. "What happened?"

He strolled away from the café entrance, along the sidewalk bordering several metal tables full of chatty, coffee-sipping patrons. Silence always paced when he "talked" on the phone. He'd had the habit in his previous life, when he had a normal voice, but now as a near-mute, he phone-paced even more, his idle energy agitated further by a hampered ability to take part in the conversation.

He kept Mr. Accord visible in his periphery.

"They..." Mrs. Enfield stopped, shuddered, cried. "They think he swallowed something, that something's stuck in his tummy."

"Will be okay."

More sobs, fading away. A sniffle. And a sigh. "I hope you're staying safe. Are you drinking?"

When Silence and Mrs. Enfield first met, when the Watchers moved him into the house next to her, it had been only a short time after C.C. had been brutally murdered. He lived a largely drunken existence in those days, and though he'd since quit binge drinking—doing so largely at Mrs.

Enfield's insistence—the old woman still monitored him, all these years later.

"Yes," Silence said.

"*Silence Jones!* What are you drinking?"

"Coffee."

A groan. "Don't sass me, boy. I'll tan your rear end as dark as mine. I don't care how old you are." She took in a deep breath, and when she spoke again, her voice had returned to melancholy. "Oh, my poor little guy! Cutting him up. They'll have to shave his belly, you know?"

"Yes."

She shuddered again. And was quiet. The phone's scratchy speaker relayed a tinny version of the sounds of the veterinarian's office waiting room—telephones, dogs barking, a receptionist calling for a patient to be seen.

She spoke again, but muffled, indiscernible, pulled away from the phone, talking to someone else.

A moment later, her voice returned with clarity and volume. "Lola wants to speak to you."

Silence didn't respond.

Ear-splitting distortion as the phone traded hands. Silence pulled his phone away from his face.

"Hi, Si."

"Hi."

"They think Baxter swallowed something." Lola's tone was more serious than it had been at Mrs. Enfield's house that morning. "Like a piece of plastic or something. They're gonna do exploratory surgery."

"I know."

"Your voice sounds a bit different to me than the last time I visited Mrs. E. Have you been doing vocal exercises? Physical therapy?"

Silence's voice did *not* sound different. It sounded like a construction foreman with a bad head cold doing a terrible Barry White impression through a scratchy, malfunctioning megaphone. As always.

Lola was just trying to spark conversation.

"No," Silence said.

Lola didn't respond immediately. Just the sound of dogs barking around her. Then she said, "I'll take good care of your neighbor. We'll keep you posted on Baxter. Goodbye, Si."

"Thanks. Bye."

He ended the call and immediately pressed the 2 button, held it for a couple of seconds—speed dial.

A Specialist answered after one ring.

Silence identified himself by codename and number. "Suppressor, A-23."

The Specialist confirmed.

"Information retrieval," Silence said and swallowed. "On the fly."

The Specialist asked if he wanted the information sent through the electronic system that Silence had already been using.

"Yes. Ray Beasley. Orlando. Former cop."

The Specialist asked if Silence suspected the former police officer of corruption or other foul play.

"Yes."

The Specialist told him information would be available in five minutes.

Silence pressed the red END button, collapsed the phone and dropped it into his pocket. He turned for the coffee shop's entrance and was two steps toward the door, when he immediately pivoted and sprinted toward Mr. Accord.

That same dark blond, curly hair he'd seen earlier through the Honda's windshield, splayed out on either side of the man's face, parted in the middle and tapered from the bottom, looking like something from the 1920s, like Charlie Chaplin. The same cleft chin, blue eyes, grim expression.

Yes, it was the man he'd seen throughout the day.

The good news was that the guy was on the same side of the highway as Silence and the coffee shop.

The bad news was he was about a block and a half away.

But Silence sprinted after him anyway.

For a moment, Mr. Accord froze on his bench, like an animal caught crossing the road, foolishly staying in place, staring at its oncoming demise. Evidently he was stunned that Silence was even making the attempt, and for half a moment, this bewilderment cemented him in place, eyes locked on Silence.

And then the man jumped off the bench and bolted away.

But his hesitation had given Silence a chance to catch up. He was still far behind the man, but he was close enough to see the details—the back of his button-up short-sleeve shirt flapping, individual strands of his curly blond hair catching the sunlight.

Ahead, the man took a corner around a Hardee's, and as Silence commanded his legs to push harder, faster, he glimpsed the area behind the restaurant—an open stretch of parking lot leading to one of the many strip malls, this one of the lower-end variety with a rundown chain hobby store and a bottom-tier home improvement store along with a hodge-podge of small shops. That big open space of parking lot would work in Silence's advantage.

He made it to the Hardee's, turned the corner...

And found nothing.

There were a lot more places for the man to have disap-peared than he'd thought. Cars and trash receptacles from a renovation project at the far side of the strip mall, which had several abandoned storefronts, all of them places for Mr. Accord to vanish.

Pursuing the man any farther was a death wish for Silence.

He straightened his sport coat. Sniffed.

And turned around.

He would let Mr. Accord come back to him.

CHAPTER SIXTEEN

JONAH CLOSED the door behind him.

A small, one-toilet bathroom. Maroon paint, low lighting. A stainless-steel handicap railing on the side wall. An over-poweringly pungent air freshener on the back of the toilet.

The floor was grimier than he would've expected from the chic coffee shop. And the mirror was littered with water spots and fingerprints. He regarded the cleaning sign-off sheet on the wall—dates and signatures. The last entry was attributed to *M. Campbell*. Campbell hadn't been taking his or her sidework seriously.

He put his hands on the cold porcelain edge of the sink, lowered his head.

He remembered what he told Brett earlier, what he'd been telling everyone for weeks—that he'd already dealt with Amber's death, already processed it inwardly because in his heart of hearts, he'd known that Amber was gone from this world.

But the part of him that *didn't* know that she had died now had confirmation.

He'd seen the outline under the drape on the stretcher. *Her* outline.

Drugs in her system...

Had it been his fault? Had Amber turned to drugs after finding out that he'd cheated on her only months earlier?

He saw it again in his mind. The blanketed shape on the stretcher. The mound at the top that would be her face. A little valley and then another mound, breasts. A longer valley that culminated at the peak at the figure's end, Amber's feet.

A shape. A figure.

A body.

Amber.

She was dead. She *was*. She really was.

She was dead.

He didn't have to tell himself that anymore. He didn't have to convince himself, to believe somehow that he had a mystical connection with Amber, that he could intrinsically sense that she'd passed.

Now he knew.

She was dead.

Jonah bent at the knees and wept.

CHAPTER SEVENTEEN

A FULL SHEET of Amber's notes. In her adult handwriting. Covering one of the blank pages at the back of *The Secret of Summerford Point*.

Gavin felt his mouth gape, and his gaze instinctively went to his brother, who had closed his eyes some time ago and hadn't reopened them. His recliner was fully laid back, and the now-empty tumbler was on the end table beside it.

For the last several minutes, Gavin had flipped through the age-brittled pages, littered with Amber's notes. Most of the notes were in her sloppy childhood scrawl, but he'd found several more in her adult handwriting sprinkled throughout. None of these made much sense to him—as they seemed highly connected to the content of the book—and none were as alarming as the first one he'd found:

I think I might be in trouble.

When he'd turned to the last page of the final chapter, he'd been frustrated—these adult notes of Amber's could be something to help him figure out what had happened to her, but there were so few of them.

That's when he'd slapped the book shut.

And gotten a glimpse of a page at the back of the book, a page the publisher had purposefully left blank, now covered with notes in Amber's adult hand.

His eyes scanned over the writing. So many notes. Amber's questions to herself. Observations. And not just her thoughts about the book.

Notes about Carlton's former police district.

District C11.

What the hell had Amber been doing?

1971 to 1982

1980 to 1984

"refined" and "crude"

Florida State Highway Patrol

Oil Man = Warren

District C11 is like Summerford

The Well

There were several instances where Amber's adult hand had mentioned the tactics that Kara, kid explorer, had used in the book, notes like:

How would Kara handle the "refined" angle?

Despite the pain, despite just finding out conclusively that

Amber had passed, Gavin smiled. Because these notes about the protagonist of a children's book exuded the personality of his niece.

This was the Amber he knew, someone who, as an adult, would still look up to the idol of her youth, seek the guidance of a literary child. Amber had a certain naïveté about her, a certain simpleness.

It was something that Gavin's brother had always hated. Carlton had been insistent that Amber grow up, mature, but Gavin appreciated her relative innocence. Purity was not a bad thing. Amber might not have been the most highly intelligent person ever, but she had heart.

But these notes... What the hell could they all mean? What was she after, and how was she connecting her father's District C11 to this children's book?

Gavin realized that in order to understand, he was going to have to read the book.

He let the pages roll over his thumb, back to the front cover. He flipped past the title page and other front matter.

And began.

Chapter 1
A Pleasant Drive in the Country

Had there ever been such a sunny day?

Well, yes, surely there had. But certainly none so delightfully cheery. And Kara just kept on smiling as she sat in the passenger seat of the car, the aromatic sea breeze tussling her hair, the sun warming her right arm and her cheeks.

Grandmother had both of the front windows rolled down. The car was a beauty with curves and smells and textures of which Kara was unaccustomed, as it was an old thing, from the 1950s, Grandmother had told her.

Goodness! The '50s! Kara hadn't even been born yet.

But the car, like Grandmother herself, had proceeded beautifully through the years, both of them clean and precise, both with a charming dignity, both having a warm, comforting presence.

Kara stuck her face closer to the open window, felt the wind on the tip of her nose, tasted the Atlantic air. The sun painted the field outside a bright green. The water sparkled beyond, a long slice of a horizon below the sapphire sky. Summerford's quaint downtown appeared in the distance, around the curve, at the bottom of the hill, right on the coastline. Little brick businesses and two-story Victorian homes, real-life dollhouses.

Yes, this was going to be a wonderful visit.

———

Gavin had been reading for half an hour. He'd smiled several times throughout, not so much because of the story itself but the memory of reading it with Amber. It was amazing how much of the story came back to him, so many years later and after having read to Amber so many *Kara* books and countless others.

The first few chapters saw Kara, kid detective, visiting her grandmother at the small seaside town of Summerford, Maine, with plans of going on many pleasant walks, many antiquing trips, and many visits to quaint restaurants and bookstores.

On her first night in Summerford, Kara and Grandmother stopped at Carlito's Café for coffee and croissants before they were to attend a play. Grandmother had excused herself to visit the restroom, at which point Kara glanced across the street and saw a sinister-looking man with a disfigured face parked in a vehicle on the opposite side of the street, twisting around in his seat to look through binoculars at the docks at the far end of town. Kara thought this quite odd, especially with the awful feeling she got from the man —his bitter expression, the slicked-back, dark hair, and a scar that traced up his left cheek, over the corner of his left eye.

At first, Kara convinced herself her imagination had gone wild again, and she chastised herself for being so judgmental. But when the man suddenly exchanged his binoculars for a camera with a long telephoto lens, Kara's junior detective instincts tingled.

The man spotted her staring in his direction, which made Kara quickly look away. Fortunately, this was right when Grandmother returned. The coffee and pastries were so delicious that Kara would have completely forgotten about the scarred man had he not driven by a few minutes later, looking in her direction with a dark stare as his car drifted past.

After the play, Kara thought she should look at what the scarred man was spying on, so, in a moment alone, she took out the opera glasses that she'd just used in the playhouse and peered down the street to the docks. The irony of using the opera glasses just as the scarred man of whom she was so suspicious had used his binoculars did not escape her.

What she saw was confusing. Police officers. But they weren't investigating; instead, they stood languidly by squad cars while civilian men loaded crates into a warehouse. Some sort of community support, no doubt. She didn't think too much of it...

Until she spotted the scarred man again

There. *At the docks.* Among the civilians, helping to unload crates.

The next day, Kara scanned the *Summerford Bugle* and found nothing about the docks. Still, something was bothering her. So that afternoon, she rode into town on the bicycle Grandmother kept for her and went to the docks.

The foreman was a shifty, crude man, very off-putting indeed, and insisted that he didn't know any scarred man or why a person like that would both spy on the docks *and* work there. One of his workers pulled him aside, out onto the floor. This left Kara alone in the foreman's office.

Opportunity had arisen.

And Kara never let an opportunity pass.

A metal tray on the foreman's desk held a stack of invoices. Kara flipped through them, found one from a company called Pearson Industries, dated the previous night, during the time the play was held. Pearson, then, was connected to the crates she'd seen.

Another invoice showing a different company, Whitehead Incorporated, bore the current date, with a time listed for that evening.

Kara slipped out before the foreman returned and went to the authorities, but she received a less than warm welcome from Summerford's Chief of Police Warren.

Which was where Gavin found himself in the story...

"And what you need to understand, little Kara, is there's an order to things. You don't just come into a police station and ask to speak directly to the chief of police. First you should have spoken to the desk sergeant, then an officer, maybe then a detective, and *only after that* I might have gotten involved. Does that make sense, sweetheart?"

He smiled at her through his big frog lips, his eyes twinkling beneath those flyaway white eyebrows.

Little Kara.

Sweetheart.

Blech!

Kara had had quite enough of his condescension. He
didn't deserve a response. Still, he was an adult, and
Kara knew proper manners, so she forced a smile.

Then she hopped out of the chair and left the office.

Gavin turned to page seventy-three, the beginning of the
next chapter, and found another one of Amber's adult notes.
A single word, featured prominently, written larger than the
others and in caps.

REFINED

Below that was an address.

941 Falconer Street

An address...

His mind flashed to the sticky note Jonah Lund and the
tall, brooding Brett had shown him. It had also born an
address.

He ran his finger along Amber's note.

Amber had been investigating C11, using *The Secret of
Summerford Point* as her guide.

But why so many addresses? Was she visiting these places?

He knew the answer.

Amber was so artless. Yet tenacious. Yet naïve. Yet
determined.

She'd been playing detective, and if she'd jotted down
addresses, the chances were high that she'd gone knocking on
doors.

Gavin made a quick decision.

He was going to Falconer Street.

CHAPTER EIGHTEEN

Silence ran a hand along his jaw, pinching the skin at the end of his chin as he studied the data on the Macintosh's monitor.

The Specialist had done well. Really well.

Footsteps behind him. He turned, half expecting to see the blond man again, Mr. Accord. His muscles flushed with adrenaline, an electric sizzle flashed over his skin, ready to pounce, even in the middle of the busy coffee shop.

But it was just Jonah.

When Silence had returned a few minutes earlier, he had found the computer station empty, just his coffee and Jonah's latte sitting on either side of the keyboard.

"You left," Silence said.

"TCB," Jonah said and sat at the stool beside him.

It was a bit of deflecting humor, calling back to the "Takin' Care of Business" poster they'd discussed earlier.

But why was he deflecting?

Silence continued to look at him, wanting further explanation.

"Come on, man," Jonah said. "I had to go to the john."

Jonah's skin was sweaty, and for a half moment, Silence took him at his word, accepting the fact that the guy really had just returned from the bathroom after suffering a sweat-inducing shit.

Then he noticed bloodshot eyes. Puffy skin beneath them. Wet cheeks, wetter than the sweat-dappled rest of his face.

He'd been crying.

And he didn't return Silence's gaze.

Silence said nothing.

He turned back to the computer. Jonah leaned over his shoulder.

The screen showed another *Defender* newspaper article, this one from 1981. But unlike the result from the newspaper's website, this was a scanned image, a digital photo of an actual newspaper, all its wrinkles and paper texture visible in a highly detailed file, a TIFF scan that had been downgraded to JPG for a smaller file size.

The headline read,

OPD Officer's Claims Disputed

Beside him, Jonah leaned in closer, squinted, his lips parting. "How did you find this?"

Silence didn't respond.

He read over the article.

ORLANDO - In the latest claim against the city's beleaguered C11 district, one officer has taken matters into his own hands.

Former Sergeant Raymond Beasley of C11 contacted the *Defender* with allegations that an internal affairs investigation he filed three months earlier was erroneously dismissed and that his insistence upon his claims led to his early termination.

Among the claims leveled by Beasley at the district are extortion, bribery, drug-trafficking, and police brutality going back at least to the late 1970s when Beasley first joined the department.

"This is just one in a long line of deceiving attacks against the officers of our district," said Lieutenant Carlton Stokes, public relations liaison for District C11. "Any wrong-doings in this group were handled decades ago. Mr. Beasley was terminated due to improper conduct, and he's either looking for revenge or a way to wipe some of the dirt off his name."

Unnamed sources verified Stokes' claims, specifying that the charges against Beasley included the use of illicit drugs.

Beasley declined to comment.

Silence leaned back, crossed his arms and stared through the image on the screen, through the monitor, through the olive-green wall, into his thoughts. The investigation's connection to Ray Beasley was something much greater than one druggie, one pervert who liked to beat up on women.

This was something bigger. And it didn't relate to Beasley. Not directly.

"Wait a minute..." Jonah said, trailing off for a moment. From the *I–think-I-see-something* tone in his voice, it was clear that he too was getting a sense of the bigger picture. "Beasley was trying to *rat out* C11. He might have been a violent drug addict, but he wasn't a crooked cop."

Silence nodded his agreement.

"So what does that mean?" Jonah said.

"Means he's in trouble," Silence said and bolted from his chair, heading for the door.

CHAPTER NINETEEN

RAY BEASLEY'S house smelled like synthetic potpourri, the kind sprayed from a can or heated in an electric lamp, one of those little plastic units that jut right out of the outlet. Cinnamon and pine. A chemical Christmas, way out of season.

To Finley, it smelled also like desperation. Like a man spraying this saccharine shit to hide a truth, a never-ending attempt to purge away what had been. The fake, manufactured quality of the scent matched everything else in the house, which had an upscale, retro vibe to it, an attempt to capture 1950s charm with 1990s-level comfort. The place stank in more ways than one.

He was in the foyer, on a patch of dark tile that had striations of lighter gray throughout, tastefully arranged to accentuate the natural imperfections. A chandelier sparkled over his head, possibly genuine crystal. In his hands was the double-barrel shotgun he'd found beside the door when he barged in.

He broke it open. Empty. Both barrels.

He scoffed and looked at Beasley, who was plastered

against the opposite wall, by the closet doors, getting as far away from Finley as he could.

"You know a gun works a lot better when it's loaded," Finley said. "What, you gonna club somebody with it?"

He swung the weapon like a club, cartoonishly, smiling.

Beasley didn't respond. His lower lip trembled.

Finley chuckled and snapped the gun back together with a *clack* that sounded off the tile, off the chandelier to the peak of the vaulted ceiling. He placed the gun where he'd found it and stepped closer to Beasley.

"Please..." Beasley said, his voice a whisper.

"Don't worry, old man. I'm not here to kill you. Can't go killing you now that you've been chatting with someone in the spotlight. Jonah Lund."

He let the name linger in the air. All its weight and implications. Waiting for Beasley to take the cue and give an explanation.

But again, the old pervert didn't speak.

"You've been out of the organization for years now," Finley said. "Because you were a goddamn rat. And you disappeared. Changed your name. But for some reason, you contacted us again. About Amber Lund. And then after the girl's found dead, suddenly the husband visits you, the guy who's keeping Amber's story in the news."

Beasley's lips shook harder, tried to form words, finally did. "She'd reached out to me. Wanted to meet up. Said she had questions only I could answer. But I ... I've never met Jonah Lund before. I'd never even heard of him before I saw him in the news."

Finley chuckled, sighed. "Really? And he just showed up at your doorstep today? He somehow found you, even after you changed your name, started a new life. *We* haven't found you all these years, but a coffee shop owner did." He paused.

"Who was the guy with him, the tall guy with dark hair? Private detective?"

"I don't know. I've never—"

"You've never seen him before either. Yes, yes."

Finley tsked, turned to the side, and when he looked back to Beasley, he brought his right hand swinging across his chest, backhanding Beasley hard enough to make him scream out, bend over, stumble to the side.

He grabbed the old bastard's shirt, pulled him back up, threw him against the wall. The bi-fold closet doors rattled. He got within inches of his face. "*What did you tell them?*"

"Nothing! I swear it!"

Finley swung a knee up, catching Beasley in the midsection. The old man folded in half, and Finley got his shin behind his knees, using his weight and momentum against him, sending him to the floor. His head snapped back, the crown striking the tile hard enough to send another sound bouncing off the walls to the peak of the vaulted ceiling. So damn hard that *Finley* felt it.

Beasley groaned, one of those terrible, guttural sounds a person makes when they've been truly wounded. In a boxing match, the announcer would be shouting, *He's hurt! He's hurt!*

Finley stepped over him, looking down with the smuggest grin he could muster. Beasley's eyes were barely open as they looked back at him, just pained slits.

"I may have been a screwup," Beasley said in a ghost of voice. "I may have been a rat. But I took down slimy little shits like you on a daily basis."

Finley sneered. "Look out, we got a tough guy here! Lying on his floor. A washed-up tough guy."

Finley kicked him in the side. The thick front edge of his Doc Martens landed squarely against his ribs.

Beasley screamed.

He kicked again, harder, the same spot. His teeth ground together, lips curled back.

Another kick. And another, rearing back like a soccer player.

And then the sound he'd been waiting for.

Snap!

Broken rib.

Beasley howled. Sobbed.

Finley breathed in. Released the tension in his face. Cleared his throat. And watched the twisting, weeping, pathetic form below him.

A disgraced cop. A druggie. A pervert. A goddamn rat. And now a beaten, worthless mound crying on the designer tile of the little life he'd tried to rebuild for himself.

Finley patted the sweat from his brow, felt a tingling sensation in his hand. Looked.

The top middle knuckle on his right hand was contused, a tight, pulsing blue knot swelling beneath the skin. He must have hit it just right when he backhanded Beasley. These things happen. He rubbed the knuckle gently, watched Beasley for another moment, then crouched beside him.

"Did you say anything that would compromise us, rat?"

"What could I say? I know nothing. I've been out for decades!"

"Then why the hell was Lund here?"

"*I don't know!*"

Beasley's eyes turned to him, still little more than slits. The left was swollen, nearly closed. All of that dig-deep bravado from his good-old-days speech moments earlier was gone. Just fear again.

Finley maintained eye contact for a long moment before speaking. "You know, I've been thinking about this all afternoon—if Ray Beasley went to the trouble of changing his name, why didn't he leave town? It's for those kids of yours, isn't it? That family you had. The wife who left you and took the two little girls."

Beasley didn't respond. His breathing grew louder.

"How old would they be now? Late teens? Twenties? That's a good age. It really is."

He gave Beasley a lopsided, dark grin. Then stood up.

"Don't you goddamn leave this townhouse. I'll be watching."

CHAPTER TWENTY

SILENCE AND JONAH moved briskly down the sidewalk. Jonah had been pissy with him since they bolted out of the Internet café.

"Man, *so what* if Beasley's in danger?" Jonah said. "He's a junkie, and he hurts women."

Silence didn't respond.

Perhaps there was something within Silence that wanted to help Beasley, more flickers of the deep compassion he'd had in his prior life. But if he was being honest with himself, Silence cared little more than Jonah did about the man's safety.

Rather, Silence wanted to find out what happened to Amber Lund, and he wanted to go home. And Ray Beasley was the key.

"I thought you're here to help find out what happened to Amber."

"I am."

"Then why the hell are we back at Beasley's?" He was shouting now. "This is a dead end!"

Silence came to a stop. Jonah continued a few steps ahead

of him before he followed suit, his shoes scuffling on the concrete.

Silence shook his head. "No. Just the opposite." He swallowed. "He's the key."

Jonah's eyebrows unknitted. His lips parted. He looked at Silence expectantly, wanting more.

So Silence added, "Beasley will lead us..." Another swallow. "To our answer."

Something deep inside Silence was talking to him, screaming at him, telling him to get to Beasley. Amber had written his name, his derogatory nickname, "Weasel," along with his prior address at the homeless shelter. After all these years. She'd reached out to him, and he hadn't been a corrupt member of C11.

Beasley was the key to it all.

Jonah's mouth opened in a kind of bewildered astonishment, as though he trusted Silence but his mind wouldn't process the fact that he might soon learn what happened to his dead wife.

There was no time to dwell. Silence brushed past him, and he was about to turn onto the sidewalk leading through the lush green lawn to Beasley's townhouse when there was a voice.

Someone shouted from behind.

He stopped. Turned.

It was Kim Hurley, the woman who'd been following them, the one who claimed she *wasn't* in cahoots with the other person following them.

And she was running right for them.

CHAPTER TWENTY-ONE

AN OPEN-AIR SPORTS bar on a sunny afternoon. There could be worse places to work.

Finley stole a look across the street at Beasley's townhouse then stepped through a wave of refreshing mist from the outdoor cooling lines in the ceiling. The main bar was on the far wall, stools with shiny plush cushions butted up against a foot rail and a high counter, big screens hanging above rows of liquor bottles. Two bartenders wearing sunglasses and green, water-stained T-shirts freshened drinks, took orders. Crowded tables, many of them outside the open retractable walls. Laughter. Cheers and jeers. A big game was playing on the screens.

He approached the hostess stand behind which a cute, short, ponytailed young woman waited, smiling. She wore a T-shirt matching the bartenders', though hers fit much tighter.

"Help you?" she said.

He gave her a grin, a sports-bar-guy grin. He could fit in well at a place like this when he needed to. Blending in with the crowd, whatever that crowd might be, was a talent he'd carefully honed. Here, he was another weekend warrior, another accountant, another Nick or Brian wanting to see the game, get a little fresh air and a beer buzz.

"Yeah," Finley said through his Brian grin. "I was hoping to get a table out..."

He trailed off.

As he was speaking, he'd turned toward the outdoor tables—one of which he wanted to snag for an unobstructed view of Beasley's place—and he'd spotted Jonah Lund and the tall guy. They were walking along the sidewalk in front of the townhouses.

And someone was running up to them, from behind, shouting for their attention.

Kim Hurley.

What the goddamn hell?

He stepped in that direction.

The hostess's voice behind him. "Were you wanting a table or ... Sir?"

Kim stopped a few feet from the other two, breathing hard. And then she just stood there in front of them, panting like an idiot, looking up at them like she wanted to say something but the words wouldn't form.

A situation was materializing, congealing before Finley's eyes. Another situation that he was going to have to take care of.

He stepped away from the hostess stand, toward the sunlight, twisting around a table, hypnotized, not believing what he was seeing.

Behind him, the hostess called out. "Sir?"

Shit!

Kim Hurley *again*.

Goddamn her.

Finley needed to do more than simply take care of this new situation.

He had to take care of *her*.

He ran out of the bar.

CHAPTER TWENTY-TWO

GAVIN VERIFIED the address written in Amber's adult handwriting at the top of page seventy-three of *The Secret of Summerford Point*.

941 Falconer Street

And then he glanced through the car window again.

A drooping signpost bore a rusted strip of green metal with the name *FALCONER STREET*.

Yes, the address was correct.

He'd arrived.

Across the street was an overpass under which was a collection of tents and other ramshackle abodes, all of it cluttered, filthy, and desperately clinging to life. Tatters of cardboard and cloth and huddled masses of people. In the back, against the embankment, was a small, decrepit building with boarded windows. A dangling cross showed that the structure had been a mission or church in a previous life.

Had Amber been here?

Here?

Not his Amber. Not Amber, with her naïveté. Amber, with her wide eyes. Amber, with her kindness.

And—as he remembered the news report—Amber, with drugs in her system.

Drugs.

Was Amber really as naïve as he remembered?

She was seventeen the last time he'd seen her. Ready for the future, her face still glowing with youth and optimism, about to pounce on the world.

Eight years ago.

A girl. A young woman but not yet an adult.

Maybe twenty-five-year-old adult Amber had come to places like Falconer Street.

And purchased drugs.

And gotten high.

He pictured a needle piercing the pale flesh at the inside of her elbow, her finger depressing the syringe's plunger.

His mind went to the note Jonah and Brett had shown him, the word at the top, the name.

Weasel

Ray Beasley. The Weasel. A former police officer who worked with Gavin's brother in District Cɪɪ. A man with a penchant for heroin and prostitutes.

Gavin searched his memory for what little else he knew about the man. Brief encounters—Christmas gatherings, summer cookouts, Amber's birthday parties. So many years ago. Before Beasley had been kicked off the force and, Gavin presumed, before his forays into illegal sex and hard drugs.

The address that had been written below "Weasel" on the sticky note—Gavin couldn't remember it, hadn't considered committing it to memory. God, he wondered if that address belonged to another shithole like this overpass. Had Amber gotten back in touch with her other "uncle," asked him to show her all the best places to get heroin?

Had Amber's life really sunk that low?

He thought of the notes Amber had written in *The Secret of Summerford Point*. She'd written "refined" twice—on page seventy-three with the address that had led him here, and also in the notes at the back of the book, where she'd written it alongside "crude."

He looked into the slum surrounding him.

Refined and crude drugs. Undoubtedly. Compliments of the Weasel.

Gavin would have thought that a destitute area like this would be the place for crude, not refined, drugs; yet her note with the address had been labeled, *REFINED*.

The Secret of Summerford Point rested in his hands. He traced along the softened edges with his thumb, savoring the visceral contrast to his surroundings.

He'd been reading for several minutes. He convinced himself that he was doing so because he needed to keep pushing through the text, had to read pages when and where he could if he was going to get to the end and learn how Amber had used this book for her investigation.

And while there was truth to that, he also knew he was procrastinating, avoiding, delaying what he had to do. Because though he was a part-time private detective and had been in more than a few sticky situations, most of his work involved unfaithful spouses, insurance fraud, and the like. He didn't delve into things like heroin sold in slums beneath overpasses.

He looked back to the book, midway down the page where he left off. The reading he'd done since parking on Falconer Street had seen Kara, kid detective, leaving the Summerford police station and later heading back to the docks for further investigation. But before she could step foot into the docks, she was confronted by the scar-faced man, who chased her through the empty nighttime streets of Summerford. The quaint town she loved so much took on a menacing ambiance when the shops were deserted, the windows were black, and she was being pursued by a sinister man.

She eluded him and thought she'd reached safety, then turned a corner and found him waiting. As he dragged her into an alley, she thought she was done for.

Only to discover that he was no villain after all.

He was an undercover agent with the FBI. His name was O'Malley. Even his scar wasn't real.

Gavin continued reading.

And as Kara looked at the bite on her fork, waiting where she kept it suspended halfway to her mouth, it certainly did look tempting, even comforting, the crust flaky and the cherries glistening. She just didn't have the appetite for it. Her stomach had been infiltrated by a most bother-some case of nerves.

O'Malley, on the other hand, had devoured his raven-ously, and as he finished his last bite, he waved the wait-ress back to the table. Nothing seemed to faze this man. Which made sense. He *was* a professional, after all.

As the waitress refilled his coffee, Kara studied the face that had seemed so very sinister earlier in the evening in the shadows. Now, in the bright lighting of the diner, the slick-backed hair seemed almost debonair, and the dark eyes were intriguing, not threatening. He was quite handsome, reminding her a bit of Father. The fake scar even looked pleasant on him, an accentuation almost.

He nodded his thanks to the waitress then turned his attention back to Kara. He took a sip of his steaming coffee and said, "The Bureau has been tracing shipments of illegal weapons making their way into the States up and down the Eastern Seaboard, even little Summerford, believe it or not, which is why I'm here undercover."

O'Malley's steady voice was calming, suddenly making her cherry pie appetizing again. She picked up her fork.

"This morning at the foreman's office, I found a pair of invoices," she said. "The first was a company called Pearson Industries."

O'Malley nodded. "That's a cover for a low-level gang out of Italy—the crates that were being unloaded last night. And the other invoice?"

"Whitehead Incorporated."

Her companion's eyes flashed over the top of his mug. "*Whitehead?*"

Kara nodded.

O'Malley slowly lowered his coffee to the table. He turned to the window, looked out into the darkness.

"What is it?" Kara said.

He turned back to her. "Whitehead is a cover for one of the world's largest illegal arms dealers." He paused, his dark eyes looking into her intently. "With Soviet ties…"

Kara gasped.

The Soviets!

O'Malley faced the window again. He ran a hand along his stubble.

And when he returned his gaze to Kara, his expression had gone even more serious. "This means Summerford is a much bigger piece of the puzzle than the Bureau has been thinking." He took a deep breath. "And I need to take action tonight."

Gavin turned the page to the next chapter, inserted the Starbucks receipt he was using as a bookmark, and put the book on the passenger seat, looked outside to the pathetic masses milling through the detritus under the overpass. Many of them now looked his way. His car wasn't necessarily a luxury machine—it was a Jeep Grand Cherokee—but it was relatively new, and he took care of it. Hell, *any* strange vehicle would raise suspicion at a place like this.

He resigned himself to the fact that he could no longer delay. He had to take action.

Slowly his hand went beneath the seat, fingers exploring until they touched cold metal. Retrieved it.

A Smith & Wesson Model 649 Bodyguard in a leather holster. A stainless-steel, .38-Special-chambered, shrouded-hammer, five-round revolver, small enough to stash in a pocket, holster and all.

He'd grown to hate it.

He hated holding it, hated seeing it, hated the responsibility of owning it.

He still enjoyed shooting it, which he'd done only at a range, never in the field. Still, those occasions had gotten more and more seldom. It had been years since he'd put a round through it.

The gun was a reminder of his brother's assessment of him. To Carlton, Gavin was a failure, a soft, bleeding-heart thinker who never became a police detective but a part-time private detective, piecing together a living through part-time gigs with his other position as an adjunct professor; a bookish weakling who hadn't even landed a wife; a poor influence for his daughter.

Gavin weighed the Smith in his palm. Exhaled. Then grabbed his olive-drab canvas messenger bag from the back seat and placed the gun and the paperback inside.

He stepped outside, locked the doors remotely with his

key fob, and pressed the button a second time to sound the horn. Just in case. Plus, they might confuse the horn's beep with the activation of an alarm system, which he didn't have —added security.

As he crossed the sidewalk on the opposite side of the street, there was the sensation of crossing a border, a boundary, a demarcation line. The further he ventured into the crumbling blacktop, the more degraded it became, the more weeds materialized, more trash. People gave him strange looks from their huddled positions next to steel drums and half-broken lawn chairs.

It occurred to him that he didn't have a plan. All he had was a word—*refined*. Who was he going to talk to? What was he going to ask?

His path pulled him toward the building in the back. Something told him that was where the action was.

A man in a bright green sweatshirt leaning against the concrete pillar closest to the building watched him approach. The man's build was hulking, and the thick, dark beard covering his cheeks was unkempt. Nonetheless, he was a bit cleaner than the people around him, and his shoulders weren't hunched with shame. He seemed like the right person to query, and when the man gave him a knowing grin, Gavin's suspicion was confirmed.

"Whatcha looking for, man?" the guy said as Gavin approached.

Gavin took a breath. Steadied himself. The point of no return.

"Refined," he said.

Gavin expected a knowing nod, maybe a coy grin. Instead, the man's eyebrows raised. "You're looking for refined? Here? This is more the place for crude, don't ya think?"

Gavin hesitated.

Maybe this was a mistake.

But he had to go with it. What choice did he have?

Point of no return indeed.

"You heard me," he said.

The other man hesitated before he responded. "You know that's not how it works, right?"

Gavin shrugged, casually, in character—the confident, composed yuppie, wondering why he was here, losing patience with a slob.

The guy stared at him for a moment, gnawed at his chapped lower lip. Traffic whizzed by above. A woman cackled in the distance.

"Give me a sec," the guy said.

He stepped away, going to the building.

The man disappeared inside. As the door shut behind the man, Gavin saw a flash of the interior—a hallway and artificial lighting. The place looked deserted, and yet it had working electricity. It was then that Gavin understood the humming sound he'd been hearing echoing off the concrete— an electric generator.

He shoved his hands in his pockets. He could feel the eyes of the homeless upon him, more of them, surrounding him. Whispers. Little snickers.

The door squeaked open, and the guy returned and walked past Gavin as he headed to his original position by the concrete post. He motioned with his head toward the building. "Go on in."

Gavin stepped past him, past more people staring at him, most of them sitting on the ground, knees to their chests, lots of them, more snickering.

He forced himself to take hold of the doorknob, which was sticky with motor oil, dust, human grime. He twisted, pushed. The hinges squeaked.

He stepped inside.

The interior was a stark contrast to the outside. The place

was no five-star hotel, but it was ... clean. It looked like the inside of a construction site trailer. Fabricated walls with molding. Indoor/outdoor carpeting. It even smelled clean, like air freshener or Lysol.

As soon as he entered, a man emerged from a doorway off the hall. White, forties, pale complexion with dark hair, a prominent Adam's apple, and eager eyes. His bright blue suit fit too baggy but looked new. The shirt beneath was dark blue and had a shine to it, satin perhaps, unbuttoned, no tie.

He walked within a couple of feet of Gavin, smiling. "So you're looking for some refined?"

Gavin nodded. "That's right."

The suited man's grin went sideways. His Adam's apple bobbed. "Coming to the source, huh?" He chuckled. "A man of discriminating taste. Well, please forgive the outside ambiance." He motioned toward the windows, the slum surrounding them visible through the thin drapes. "We usually deliver, as you know."

"My eyes aren't so delicate," Gavin said.

The suited man grinned broader. "My man." A discerning pause as the man stroked his short beard, still smiling, but his eyes narrowing a bit. "There are only two available. I mean, you didn't give us any notice."

"It's fine."

Another pause. "Well, come on, then."

The man put a hand on Gavin's shoulder, led him down the dark hallway, opened the last door, and motioned for Gavin to step past him into the room, which he did.

A stark office with a cheap desk, befitting the construction site trailer vibe. Lining the walls were simple steel chairs with brown cushions.

Two of the chairs were occupied—women dressed in expensive but quite short, quite revealing dresses. Immaculate hair. Perfect makeup. Every bit of them was ready for a sophisticated cocktail party, their sultry opulence glaringly out of place in the surroundings.

Refined.

Gavin wasn't being sold refined drugs.

He was being offered high-end prostitution.

CHAPTER TWENTY-THREE

KIM HURLEY STOOD A FEW AWAY, not looking at them, twisting a ring around her pinky, chewing on her lip.

"Talk," Silence said.

She looped the ring over her finger once more, then glanced up at him. "I, um, followed you here earlier."

"I know."

She wasn't nearly as good at following someone as Mr. Accord.

"I saw that it was Ray Beasley you were talking to here." She pointed to the townhouse. "You need to know something. He wasn't involved in Amber's death."

Silence's suspicion was confirmed.

There had been something about Beasley when Silence first met him, something in his demeanor, his appearance that said the man wasn't connected to Amber's demise.

But somehow Beasley was involved in the big picture.

Silence turned to Jonah, found his eyes waiting on him.

Jonah then inched closer to Kim. "How do you know that?"

Kim went back to twisting her ring. Her attention drifted

away from them again, to Beasley's townhouse. "I know because *I* was involved in her death."

Silence didn't turn to look at Jonah, but he heard his reaction, an audible gasp.

"Look, C11 is corrupt," Kim said. "Everybody knows that. But it's not just another backslapping, bribe-taking bunch of crooked cops. It's so much bigger." She took a deep breath, steadying her resolve. "They run a prostitution ring. It's called the Well. They give these girls an option: get arrested and go to jail, maybe prison, or join the Well. High- and low-end call girls. 'Refined' and 'crude' are the terms they use."

She scoffed, chewed her lip harder, vigorously, like a worn-out piece of chewing gum.

Something else was about to come out of her, something she was fighting on the inside.

She took another deep breath.

"I'm one of the refined," she said quietly.

Thoughts fluttered through Silence's mind, joining magnetically, only to form a vortex that funneled back into the depths of doubt, the sole thread of cogent thought, the only connecting element being Amber Lund.

Amber, the dead woman, the daughter of a disappointed father, a father who was a part of a corrupt police division, one running a prostitution ring.

Amber, who was conducting an investigation of her father's police division, searching for her long-lost surrogate uncle, a man who was also involved in the division.

Amber, who was found with drugs in her body.

Amber, whose best friend was a prostitute.

He looked at Jonah.

Amber, whose love of her life had betrayed her.

She was a woman whose emotional life had been in shambles, right after she was married, right after things were supposed to get better for her. Maybe she'd turned to the world of her father, a dark, corrupt world full of drugs and illegal sex. Silence had seen it before, both in his previous life as a police officer and certainly in his current life as a vigilante assassin—people hitting rock-bottom, self-destructing within the patterns they'd been exposed to all their lives, when there seemed to be no other choice.

His attention strayed over Jonah's shoulder to Beasley's picture-perfect townhouse beyond.

Beasley. The key to it all. The person who would lead Silence to the answers about Amber.

And even though Beasley might have been a piece of shit, the bastard was in trouble. Plus, it certainly seemed like the guy had turned his life around.

For that reason alone, aside from the fact that he was the key to the investigation, Beasley was worth saving.

Kim spoke again. "And I—"

"Hold that thought," Silence said.

He dashed toward Beasley's front door. A moment later, he heard Jonah and Kim run after him.

At the porch, he put his finger on the doorbell. Stopped. He'd heard something. On the other side of the door. Footsteps. At a run.

Silence pounded on the door.

A shadow flashed across the glass of the peephole.

The door swung open. Beasley stared out at them, looking terrified. He'd taken a beating, his left eye swollen shut.

"You can't be here," he said.

"Why?"

"Because he's here. I ... I think he's here again. I heard something ... out back ... just before you knocked."

"Who?"

"Oh, God. Did you hear that? He's back. You have to leave! He thinks I'm working with you."

Beasley went to shut the door. Silence threw his hand into the gap, the edge of the door thudding to a halt in his palm.

"*Who?*"

"I don't know. Some guy. Some enforcer. From the Well."

A face flashed through Silence's mind. The blond, curly-haired man, the one who'd been following them all day.

Silence had no more time for questions, delays. He shouldered the door hard, slamming Beasley back. His shoes squeaked on the tile of the entranceway.

He drew his Beretta from the shoulder holster.

"Get out," he said.

"I can't leave! He told me I can't. He threatened my daughters!"

Silence had even less time to argue. If there really was someone in here, not only was Beasley's life in danger, but now so was Silence's.

He looked out the door. Jonah and Kim stood on the doorstep, both wide-eyed.

If Beasley was correct and this enforcer was here—

A sound. From upstairs.

Silence bolted to the side, grabbed the handrail, bounded up the steps, three at a time.

To the second floor. Plush carpeting. Built-in shelving on the far wall, loaded with brushed nickel picture frames, photos of Beasley's daughters. Three doorways. One open, two closed.

Another noise. This one from the ground floor.

Shit.

A violent shuffle. A muffled scream of pain. Another scream, this one from outside the townhouse.

Kim.

Covering himself with the Beretta, Silence returned to the stairwell, cleared the corner, looked down.

And saw Beasley.

On the floor.

Throat slashed. A massive pool of blood spreading on the tile surrounding him. Coughing, blood spouting from his mouth.

Silence leaned over the handrail, looked through the open doorway.

The other two were gone.

Where Jonah and Kim had stood moments earlier, there was now just brickwork and white vinyl railing, bathed in bright sunlight.

Down the stairs. A glance to Beasley. He was nearly expired. Another glob of blood shot from his mouth. His breathing crescendoed. A gurgling exhale. And his head rolled to the side.

The last few steps. Silence swept his Beretta before him, clearing the threshold. To the door. He looked back at Beasley.

Yes, quite dead.

For a brief moment, Silence had seen light on the horizon, answers about Amber Lund's fate, a resolution to the chaos.

And just like that, his hopes were expired. They drowned in the pool of blood spreading on the tile around Ray Beasley's lifeless neck.

Well, shit.

He cleared the doorway. Looked outside.

And saw the man who'd been following them all day.

The curly-haired, blond man, on the far side of the long lawn that fronted the townhouses, running down the sidewalk to the Honda Accord and clutching Kim's wrist. She stumbled behind him, screaming.

Jonah was just behind them, in pursuit. He grabbed Kim by the free arm, tried to pull her from the man's grasp, but Mr. Accord sidestepped, slugged Jonah across the jaw. A wet, dull *crack*, and Jonah collapsed.

Shouts, screams from the sports bar. A few good Samaritans dashed across the street toward the chaos.

Mr. Accord threw Kim into the car through the driver side, and with a quick, practiced motion, he was immediately behind the wheel. The Accord fired up, the tires chirped, and the car zoomed off just as the good Samaritans ran up.

Silence sprinted up to Jonah, splayed on the sidewalk, eyes squinting.

"Keys," Silence said.

Jonah didn't respond, either hesitant or dazed from the blow.

"*Keys!*"

Jonah complied, digging in his pocket and holding the keys up to him.

Silence snatched them from his hand, already reaching a run once more. The Fiero was ahead, a block away, a splash of faded red paint. A few strides of Silence's long legs and he was there. Door unlocked. Into the driver's seat. A look through the windshield.

Ahead, the Accord screeched around a corner, disappeared behind a squeaky-clean hardware store bounded by a line of oversized terra cotta pots brimming with flowers.

Silence fired the engine, which belched out its stank again. He slammed the stick into first, dropped the clutch, and the Fiero hurdled off.

CHAPTER TWENTY-FOUR

FINLEY LOOKED to the rearview mirror as he flew down the street, pressing the gas pedal harder.

No Fiero.

But he'd seen the tall man run to the car, hop in. And just before Finley had taken the corner, the Fiero had rocketed in his direction.

Finley jerked the Accord to the side when a hatchback backed onto the street from a parking lot, not noticing the other vehicle coming right at it, going twice the speed limit.

Kim screamed again. Whiny bitch.

"Slow down!" she screeched.

"Shut up."

Finley yanked the steering wheel, whipping around a pickup truck parallel parking, its backup lights aglow, which sent the Accord toward the opposite side of the road, where a trio of women stepped off the sidewalk, about to cross the street. They pulled back, screamed.

Kim screamed too.

Finley maneuvered the Accord around the women, their arms interlocked protectively, bewildered faces, saucer eyes.

"What the hell is this, Finley?" Kim said. She had both hands clenched on the passenger seat cushion, eyes straight forward and wide.

Finley didn't answer. He checked their six.

There it was.

A streaking red splash in the rearview mirror.

The Fiero peeled around the corner he'd just taken. The tall man loomed in the driver's seat, his dark hair, the dark void of his eyes on a face that was tilted forward, determined, both hands gripping the steering wheel.

Shit.

The gap between the cars was shrinking. Rapidly.

This guy could drive.

Shit, shit, shit.

"Where are you taking me?" Kim whined.

"I said *shut up!*"

Another corner, just ahead and to the left. The one he'd been anxiously waiting for.

The corner that might get him out of this mess.

Finley wrenched the steering wheel. The force threw him into Kim's shoulder and plastered Kim to the passenger door. More screams. The Accord shuddered, tires squealed.

He smashed the gas pedal, stole a glance at Kim, who was scrambling to fasten her seatbelt.

The Fiero closed in, filling the rearview.

CHAPTER TWENTY-FIVE

Silence watched the Accord turn.

And he cursed.

Because the blond man had just given himself a major tactical advantage. He'd entered an urban hedge maze.

An auto salvage yard.

A sprawling affair with hundreds of vehicles. And it wasn't one of those nice, corporate chain, you-pull-it sort of places with rows of evenly spaced vehicles organized by make in fields of thick gravel. No, this was a real-deal, old-school behemoth with corroded piece-of-shit vehicles piled on top of each other in teetering towers that surely violated any number of municipal codes. Tires and sheets of rusty metal. Barely maintained paths riddled with oil-slicked puddles.

The Accord flew into the lot, between two of the car towers. It immediately turned right, disappearing.

Silence hit the brake, downshifted, brought the Fiero into the lot, and immediately was jolted hard, his teeth cracking into each other. Water fanned out of the pothole he'd struck. The impact made an awful noise from the Fiero's undercarriage. A pang of guilt. You don't hurt a guy's car. He'd reimburse Jonah if there was any damage.

Second gear. A surge of gas. A high-pitched whine as the tires spun momentarily before grabbing hold. A man in coveralls appeared from behind one of the vehicles, screaming at him, waving his arms, pissed off. He jumped back when Silence zoomed the Fiero past him.

No sign of the Accord.

He peeled left, around the skeleton of a Pinto. Another empty path in front of him, long and muddy.

Around a pile of tires and rims.

Another empty pathway.

He turned again.

Nothing. No Accord. Just a father and son prying an alternator from an Oldsmobile and staring at him in confusion.

Silence eased his foot onto the brake, dropped a gear, slowed the Fiero.

And exhaled.

Dammit.

He gave the father and son a snappy wave as he passed and then turned left, heading toward the exit. Though his circuitous path had taken him deep into the belly of the automotive graveyard, his rigorous training ensured he'd maintained his bearings. He knew which way to go to get out.

Goddamnit.

He'd lost them.

And, as if on cue, he glimpsed the street through a gap in the spires of rusty metal and saw the Accord, far away, taking off, its engine roaring.

CHAPTER TWENTY-SIX

PROSTITUTION.

Oh, God. That's what all this was about.

Amber had been trying to become a high-end prostitute.

Gavin had to stay in character, but standing there in that horrid office with the grinning creep and the two prostitutes leering at him, the realization that Amber had been pursuing this life nearly made his knees give out.

It all added up...

The revelation she'd gotten from her husband, two weeks after marrying him, the devastation she must have felt.

The word refined.

Her search for the Weasel, her other "uncle," the one who liked hookers.

The drugs in her system, probably heroin like Uncle Weasel's drug of choice.

And though Gavin's mind had formed the dark connections, forcing him to picture his niece here in this creepy building, this ramshackle structure that had been renovated into a hooker office, his impulses quickly brought his thoughts away from Amber and to self-preservation.

Because Gavin had to get the hell out of there.

If Amber had gotten herself in way too deep, he'd gotten himself in equally deep by following her footsteps.

The door was still open behind him. But before he could turn, there was a noise.

A man approached, stopped in the doorway. He was black, on the short side, wearing a gray T-shirt peppered with holes, a pair of soiled jeans. And a grin.

"Like your options?" the man said, tilting his head toward the prostitutes.

Gavin looked at the women again. They both gave him salacious bats of their eyes. One of them made a crude gesture.

Gavin glanced at the man behind him, then to the suited man. "You know, with all respect to the ladies, this just isn't what I had in mind."

The women pouted.

Gavin inched toward the door.

The man in the doorway gave a suspicious look to the suited man, who then stepped closer to Gavin.

"You a cop?" the suited man said.

Before Gavin could reply, the other man closed in as well, drew a pistol.

Gavin gasped.

The man patted him down, found Gavin's gun and the book, which Gavin had put in his back pocket.

The man stowed Gavin's Bodyguard then held the book at arm's length, squinting at the title. "What the hell? A damn kids' book."

The suited man joined him in a laugh.

Then the black guy's expression suddenly changed, his cheeks going slack. He'd turned back the front cover—and noticed something.

"Amber Stokes," he read from the first page. He glanced

up at the suited man. "As in, Amber Lund, that missing girl. They just found her dead!"

"I know, goddamnit," the other one said. He faced Gavin but continued talking to his associate. "This guy *is* a cop. "

Gavin tried to say something, couldn't. Sweat flushed his palms. His leg muscles tightened.

And he thought again of Carlton's assessment of him. Gavin was living up to every insult his brother had ever hurled at him—the weakling, the poser, the man in over his head.

"A cop??" the black guy said. He lowered his gun. His free hand went up, fingers spreading as far as his eyes had gone wide. "Listen, man, I told that Amber chick when she was here that we don't know nothing."

Gavin found his voice.

"So she *was* here." He pointed at the hookers. "Looking to join, yes?"

"What? No, man, she wasn't trying to join. She was just asking about the Oil Man."

The term resonated with Gavin.

Oil Man.

Amber's notes, the list in the back of the book. There had been one that said:

Oil Man = Warren

Warren was the fictional police chief of Summerford, but clearly the Oil Man was real.

There had been a note that referred to *The Well*. And, of course, *refined* and *crude*. Code words, prostitution labels traded out for petroleum terms.

The Oil Man must have been the head of the operation.

"But I swear," the black guy continued, "that's all I told her, and—"

"Shut up!" the white one yelled. "Don't tell this asshole anything."

"Dude's a cop!" the other one insisted. "And he's investigating Amber Lund."

The suited one narrowed his eyes, stepped closer to Gavin.

"No. He's no cop. Cops carry badges. They have to. This one's a private investigator. Aren't you?"

Gavin's heart thundered in his chest.

The suited man motioned for his associate, who closed in on Gavin from behind.

The prostitutes lost their salacious grins. They hopped from their chairs and hurried to the back corner of the room, high heels thumping on the thin carpet, and crouched behind the desk, preparing for something bad.

"Yeah, this guy's a private eye," the suited man continued. A dark smile flashed over his face. "And no one's gonna come looking for him."

CHAPTER TWENTY-SEVEN

SILENCE GRIPPED the sticky vinyl wrapping on the steering wheel as the Fiero hurtled down the street, back to Beasley's townhouse.

Ahead, Jonah sat on the sidewalk, knees at his chest, arms wrapped around them, a small crowd of helpful individuals gathered nearby.

Silence zipped past the group, reached his left hand to the side of his seat, and tugged the parking brake. The Fiero screamed as it swung around to the opposite direction. He pushed back against the wave of centrifugal force, shoving both hands against the steering wheel, pressing his back into the musty seat, stabilizing himself. Screams from the group surrounding Jonah.

He burped the gas, pulled the Fiero to the curb, brought it to a screeching halt right by the crowd, who stepped away, some of them jeering at him. He popped the passenger door open, revealing Jonah, who stared at him slack-jawed.

"Get in," Silence said.

Jonah reluctantly, painfully pulled himself off the concrete and climbed into the passenger seat.

As soon as he was in, Silence dropped the clutch, and the Fiero shot off, not even giving Jonah a chance to shut the door. The car's momentum did the trick, shutting the door with a loud *thud*. Jonah yanked his arm and leg out of the way.

He then leaned his head back against the headrest, closed his eyes, groaned.

"I'm doing fine," he said. "Thanks so much for asking."

"Hear?" Silence pointed upward. Sirens. In the distance, getting louder. He swallowed. "No time for self-pity."

"Of course," Jonah said, touching the bloody bulge on the side of his head. "How silly of me."

Silence took the next corner hard, around the block of townhouses, shifting Jonah in the passenger seat.

After another few feet, he pulled the Fiero around another corner, just as aggressively, into the alley between the opposite-facing rows of houses.

Jonah's mouth fell open as he looked out the window. "What the hell are you doing?? Cops are coming!"

Silence didn't respond. He leaned over the steering wheel and looked out beneath the top edge of the windshield, found the right building, brought the car to a sudden stop that sent Jonah into the dash.

He put the stick in neutral, yanked the parking brake, and stepped outside, leaving the engine running.

While the fronts of the townhouses were unique, the unified backside of the connected homes was a long stretch of sameness—pure white broken up by windows and back-doors with stairs.

Silence ran up a set of steps, climbed to a door beneath a portico.

The sound of the passenger door shutting. Jonah's voice behind him. "Brett!"

Silence tried the door. Locked. With no time for anything subtler, he kicked. Hard. The doorframe splintered violently, loudly, spiky fingers of freshly shorn wood fanning out from the impact. The door smacked into the interior wall.

"Holy shit," Jonah uttered.

Inside, down the long central hallway to Beasley's body in the foyer. Silence went to the console table that ran along the staircase, pointed at Beasley.

"Check him."

"*For what?* Dude's dead."

"Cellular phone."

And when Jonah hesitated, Silence added, "Do it."

Silence would leave that task to Jonah. There was a more daunting one for Silence to consider.

The console table had a phone, a little glass lamp, a small drawer. But no notepad, no sticky notes, no paper of any sort.

He went down the hall, his footfalls pounding against the hardwood floor, the wail of the sirens insistent between each footstep.

The sirens were louder, closer.

And Jonah had heard them. "They're gonna be here any minute!" he called from the other end of the hall.

Silence threw open one of the white panel doors. A little bathroom. Reeked of potpourri and cleaner.

Next door. This was it, what he was looking for. The office—stately wooden desk, bookshelves, a filing cabinet.

He fell into the overstuffed leather chair.

The sirens rang in his ears.

Nothing on the surface of the desk, which was covered by a sheet of glass.

Jonah walked up behind him, hands empty, no cellular phone. "Hurry up, man!"

Top drawer. Pens, pencils. Two pads of sticky notes. He thumbed through both of them. Blank. Letters addressed to Beasley—electric and water bills.

He opened a side drawer. Tape. Stamps. A box of envelopes.

The sirens screamed down the hall.

Right outside.

Jonah bounced on his feet beside him.

Another drawer. A small notebook. Silence flipped it open. A few pages of handwriting, numbers, some simple math, possibly figuring out his bills. A grocery list.

He flipped the page. And saw something.

Something so significant it made his fingers fan wide in response.

Beasley had written:

- *come alone*
- *be ready to tell all*
- *941 Falconer Street*
- *Carlton will be there*

Carlton...

So, Beasley had recently contacted Carlton Stokes.

And yet he'd been out of touch with Carlton and the rest of C11 for years, even changed his name.

Why were they talking now?

Jonah smacked his back. "*Come on!*"

The sirens wailed outside.

And stopped.

Shouting. Footsteps. The cops were charging into the house.

Silence grabbed the notepad.

They sprinted from the room, down the hall, and through the back door, which squealed on its ravaged hinges.

As he ran down the steps to the Fiero, Silence heard more shouting from the house as the cops found Beasley.

"Sir! Sir, can you hear us!??"

No, folks, Silence thought, *he certainly can't hear you.*

Into the Fiero. Silence threw the stick into first, and they pulled off.

CHAPTER TWENTY-EIGHT

Damn, Finley hated this place.

The shantytown at the overpass on Falconer Street at Blair. The place literally smelled like shit, and the bums that inhabited it reminded Finley of the life from which he'd worked so hard to break free. Yet to escape these people's fate, he had to spend a considerable amount of time around them, given how often he had to come to the unassuming old building that served as the Well's headquarters.

He wasn't sure if that was irony, but whatever it was, he didn't like it.

Traversing through this disgusting trashcan of human existence was something he had to do to maintain this second chance he'd been given. Finley was a very fortunate man. He reminded himself regularly. It got him through the times he had to visit this shithole.

He had Kim by the arm, and since they'd gotten out of the car, her whining had intensified. She was also turning a lot of the bums' heads. They leered at her, wicked smiles full of rotten teeth. There were catcalls. And some vulgarities.

Finley had to admit that Kim's trim figure, nicely curved

hips, pleasant breasts, and pouty lips weren't bad on the eyes. She was attractive in a mopey, my-parents-didn't-give-me-everything-I-wanted-so-I'm-gonna-get-back-at-them-by-being-a-literal-whore sort of way.

Ahead, Shaw was at his station, leaning against the column closest to the building, and as Finley and Kim drew nearer, he pushed off the column, held his head up professionally, straightened his bright green sweatshirt as one would a suit jacket. Pathetic. Like all the other low-level workers in the Well. Finley was proud of how quickly he'd climbed the ranks, but the competition wasn't exactly stiff.

Finley knew more about Shaw than Shaw would have wanted him to, more than he probably even thought possible. Finley knew Shaw had been in and out of prison for most of his twenties. B&Es. Grand larceny. Forged credit cards. Finley also knew that Shaw was apprehended after a murder in District C11, and while the police report stated that Shaw was simply in the area, Finley knew the reality—that Shaw had been seen hovering over the body with a bloody knife. Shaw was never tried, never even arrested, and now he was muscle for the Well, like Finley, except at a much lower station.

Shaw was a piece of shit. Fat and hairy. Smelly. The kind of guy you imagine watching TV all day, eating Cheetos and ice cream and getting high in three different ways. Finley wagered he was a pervert, one with a small, sweaty dick.

A disgusting waste of humanity.

Shaw gave another tug to his oil-stained green sweatshirt and waddled up to Finley. "We got trouble."

Finley didn't respond, just brought Kim to a halt and looked at Shaw, waited for him to continue. He wasn't wasting any breath on a man like Shaw.

"This guy came here," Shaw continued, "looking for some refined." He held up his walkie-talkie. "They just phoned me, told me to watch the door." He looked over his shoulder.

"Something's going down. They think the guy's a private detective."

Finley glanced at the building.

"Shit."

People didn't come directly to the Well's office looking for refined. Something wasn't right.

It couldn't be the big guy or Jonah Lund. Finley had come here directly from Beasley's neighborhood; they couldn't have beaten him here. And anyway, how would they know about this place?

But this had to somehow be related to them...

Or Kim.

He turned to her—the bitch who'd been following Jonah Lund and his associate, the bitch who'd contacted them *twice.*

He pointed to the building. "Who is it, Kim? Another friend of yours?"

She shook her head with that pathetic, scared look on her face.

"Right..." Finley said.

He gave things another moment of consideration. Then pulled Kim's arm, shoving her to Shaw. She yelped.

"Get her to the van," Finley said. "And keep her there. Zip-tie her. Knock her ass out if you have to. The Well has been compromised. I'm gonna get her to the boss."

Shaw hesitated. It wasn't a moment of insubordination— Shaw wouldn't dare stand up to Finley—but a moment of stunned confusion.

Then he nodded and tugged Kim away.

Finley started toward the building.

A sharp, loud noise cracked through the overpass, making several of the bums cry out in surprise. Glass. Something shattering. Something big.

One of the building's windows.

Finley went into a full sprint.

CHAPTER TWENTY-NINE

GAVIN CRASHED THROUGH THE WINDOW.

A sudden change in environment. One moment he was struggling with the thugs in the shitty little office—and impressed with himself for how well he'd fought them off—and the next moment, after letting his guard down briefly, after an electric jolt of pain as his head crashed through the glass, he was outside. Halfway. To his waist. Out in the slum again. The smell of burning paper, garbage. Screams from several of the homeless.

Tugging on his shirt. A jolt of momentum. And he was back in the office.

More screaming. Not from the homeless but from the high-class hookers cowering behind the desk.

The black guy had Gavin by the legs. The suited white guy had him by the shoulders. Gavin's face was tight and burning from the blows he'd received.

The three of them tumbled to the thin, rough carpeting, a tangle of legs and grasping arms.

Something glistened. A shard of glass, still connected to a chunk of the window frame. Gavin grabbed it by the wooden section, swung in a broad arch, catching the white guy across the face.

The man screamed. A trail of blood slung onto the wall. One of the women screeched.

Gavin shook the black guy off his legs, got behind the man's knees, twisted, and threw him into a rolling pile, sending him to the opposite wall.

And there it was.

His gun, the Bodyguard, still in its holster a few feet away.

When the two men had first converged on Gavin, he'd been able to wrench the black guy's pistol from his hands, sending it through the open doorway and into the hall. In the ensuing scuffle, his own gun, the Bodyguard, had fallen from the man's pocket and skittered to the side.

All through the exchange of blows, the three men had stolen anxious glances at the Bodyguard, just out of reach on the other side of the room. Someone was going to grab it, and when he did, that man would have the power.

It was a few feet away, by the wall, on the other side of the room. Gavin dove for it.

But he stopped short, abruptly, his flight suddenly halted. Something had grabbed him from behind. He crashed to the floor hard, sending a jolt through his ribs.

He looked back. The black guy had him by the ankles, his face covered with sweat and twisting in fury.

The Bodyguard was tantalizingly close.

Inches away.

Gavin reached out; his fingers touched it.

Then he heard something.

Beside him. At the doorway.

He looked up.

A man stood over him, someone he hadn't yet seen.

Blond curly hair, parted in the middle.

He pointed a pistol at Gavin's face.

CHAPTER THIRTY

JONAH STRUGGLED to keep up with Brett's long strides as they ventured farther into an area of homeless people, the address from Beasley's notes, some sort of ragtag community of tents and cardboard boxes, blankets and old mattresses. The smell was overpowering, a mixture of human filth, bonfires, and industrial waste.

Brett led them to a building in the back, something dilapidated yet clearly important. Boards covered the windows. A dark rectangular area on the wall beside the main door had evidently held a sign at one point in time. Beneath that was a cross, hanging askew.

There was a shout from the left. "Hey!"

A fat guy in a bright green sweatshirt standing beside a white panel van at the cross street. He slid the van's side door shut with a thunk, then waved his hands, looking right at Jonah and Brett. The driver's side door was open, and he shut and locked it before lumbering over at a slow jog, dodging tents and huddled forms.

When the guy reached them, he put his hands on his waist, chest heaving, head angled back, sucking in air.

"Shop's closed for the day," the man said between breaths.

Jonah turned to see Brett's reaction. Which was a non-reaction. Brett just pivoted and started for the building again.

The man grabbed Brett's arm, and in a blur, the hand was gone. Brett had swiped it away so fast, Jonah had hardly seen the motion.

Another one of Brett's bizarre skills that seemed to materialize out of nowhere, skills that made Jonah realize Brett was a lot more than what he had originally taken him for.

Again, Jonah wondered if he was some sort of government operative.

Open-mouth wonder replaced the sloppy man's anger, and it took him a moment to regain his courage.

"I said, shop's closed. Your buddy's already been here, the guy with the beard."

Brett looked at Jonah then.

"Gavin..." Jonah said.

Brett nodded. He turned back to the guy in the sweat-shirt. "When was he here?"

"Man, piss off. Get out of here."

Brett jabbed him in the throat.

Once more, the movement was so fast that Jonah hardly perceived it.

Efficient and flawless. Yet brutal. Violence that leaves an echo.

The man wheezed, bent over.

"Talk," Brett growled.

The man's hands were on his knees. "He's..." Wheeze. "He's still here."

The man pointed to the boarded-up building with the crooked cross.

Brett started toward the building again, this time running. Jonah sprinted after him.

And as they ran, Brett reached beneath his jacket and

retrieved a black pistol. A moment later, he took out a small metal tube. A silencer. He screwed it onto the end of the pistol.

Holy shit...

They made it to the building.

"Stay outside," Brett said.

Brett kicked in the door as he had at Beasley's. No hesitation. Effortlessly powerful. The decaying doorframe exploded. The door flew in.

Beyond the entrance was a hallway.

And in that hallway, a staggering sight.

Gavin Stokes. Bloodied. Surrounded by three other men.

Including the blond-headed man, who had a gun aimed at Gavin.

CHAPTER THIRTY-ONE

FOUR MEN in the hallway in front of Silence. Centered in the group, a gun to his head, was Gavin Stokes.

Silence's thoughts slowed.

An engine powering down. The last bit of steam whistling out of a kettle. A baseball rolling to a stop in thick grass.

Things became quiet.

C.C. had always told Silence that his mind was chaotic, and she helped him with methods of sorting his thoughts, calming the anxieties, soothing the storm of activity within his brain. Things like mind mapping, meditation, deep breathing. The techniques had become a toolbox from which he could grab the necessary piece of mental equipment for a specific application.

Through the years, the constant use of those C.C. teachings had led to a cumulative effect, one that came out when adrenaline was flowing the fastest, an immediate internal response to chaos in the external. In moments like these, time slowed, his reactions became molecularly precise, he saw and heard everything, he existed in a vacuum of time, a vortex of space, and all was still.

When paired with the brutal coaching he'd received from Nakiri, his trainer when he was first conscripted into the Watchers, the stillness that had developed from C.C.'s Zen-filled teachings took on a whole new function.

It became a lethal weapon.

The curly-haired man, Mr. Accord, in front of Gavin, a Heckler & Koch P9S in his hand, pointed at Gavin's face.

Gavin, head arched back, tendons bulging from his neck.

Two other guys. Behind Gavin. One with a long gash across his cheek, blood pouring onto a baggy blue suit.

The other in a gray T-shirt, jeans, grabbing Gavin from behind, fingers yanking his hair.

Mr. Accord's eyes had found Silence's in the fraction of sluggish time when the door had burst open, a look of recognition, confusion, dread.

Mr. Accord kept his pistol on Gavin, but in that sliver of a moment, Silence sensed danger from the man's associates, two electric blips in the quiet nothingness.

They both leveled guns in Silence's direction.

Silence's arm raised, going to the left.

He fired.

Striking the suited one, through the shoulder.

The Beretta shifted six inches to the right. Fired.

The round cut through the other man's neck. An explosion of blood. A wet scream.

Mr. Accord had pulled Gavin in front of him. A human shield. He moved toward the side door.

The bodies fell.

First the suited one. Then the one in the gray T-shirt.

Gavin, too, fell. To his knees. A flash behind him, and Mr. Accord vanished.

Two steps. Silence was beside Gavin, aiming the Beretta downward, at the enemy who was still alive, the suited one.

Another round through the center of the forehead. The man's eyes remained open, mouth as well.

The Beretta swept to the side. To the other man. The throat wound was catastrophic. He was very much dead.

Silence put a round through his forehead anyway.

A delayed double tap.

You can never be too sure.

Sounds seemed louder. The air felt warmer, more real. Time returned to him.

It had all happened in a couple of seconds.

He leapt over Gavin, pressed himself against the wall, threw open the side door, swept his gun across the threshold.

No curly-headed bastard. But an infinite number of nooks and crannies for him to have disappeared into—tents and boxes and shopping carts and dozens of homeless people.

Mr. Accord was gone.

Silence returned to Gavin, who stared in disbelief at the bodies lying next to him. "Holy shit, man! *Shit!* Holy shit! What are you?"

Silence offered his hand, pulled him to his feet.

The roar of a gunshot.

An explosion beside them, at the floor, inches away from Gavin's foot.

Chunks of wood, strips of carpet shot to the ceiling.

Mr. Accord...

He was beneath the building.

"Come on!" Silence said.

They ran for the door.

CRACK!

Another shot. A couple of feet behind them. Silence felt the tremor through the soles of his shoes.

A yard from the door.

CRACK!

This one blew particles between his jacket and his shirt, peppering his back with stings.

Outside, Jonah stared at Silence through the open doorway, mouth slack, cheeks pallid.

"Run!" Silence shouted, a painful tear in his monstrous throat.

Jonah turned, sprinted off.

CRACK!

Through the doorway, into the homeless camp. Frightened people staring in his direction, pointing.

Jonah running ahead of him. Gavin struggling a few feet behind.

Silence looked back.

Mr. Accord was on his stomach, in the open space between the building and the earth, emptying a magazine from the bottom of his HK, grabbing another from his pocket.

Shit.

"Go! Go!"

CRACK!

A bullet whistled past. People screamed. They scattered in all directions.

CRACK! CRACK!

A woman in front of them took a round to the back, dropped.

Silence ran to the side, behind one of the massive concrete uprights. Jonah and Gavin followed suit.

CRACK! CRACK!

More rounds screamed past. One of them struck the upright with a solid *thwack*.

The street was ahead. There was the Fiero.

Which was a two-seat vehicle.

Two seats. Three men. A major tactical disadvantage in a situation like this.

Silence was just about to dash toward the Fiero, planning to figure it out when they got there, when Gavin darted in front of him.

"Come on!" Gavin said and went toward a green Jeep Grand Cherokee.

Silence and Jonah followed.

More screaming. People bashed into Silence from all sides.

The smell of bonfires. Urine.

The shots rained from the building.

CRACK! CRACK! CRACK!

Another homeless person took a hit, a man in his fifties, a brutal head wound that took off his toboggan hat and a chunk of his skull.

They made it to the Jeep. Silence threw open the passenger door, got in, closed it, crouched beneath the window.

Gavin got behind the wheel. Jonah was in the back.

Gavin threw the Jeep into gear, and they screeched off, dodging people as they scattered across the street.

CHAPTER THIRTY-TWO

A HALF HOUR after the pandemonium at Falconer Street, Finley found himself in an entirely different environment.

A guest room in a suburban home.

A nice bedspread, light blue with stripes, clean and new. Dark blue drapes, pulled tight, and a fancy vase, also dark blue, filled with frilly ornamentation of some sort. A dresser with knickknacks, arranged just so. A small lamp throwing light into the darkened room.

And on the bed, her wrists and ankles zip-tied, was Kim Hurley.

"You know, Kim, in one way or another, all of this is your fault," Finley said.

She squirmed in her binds. "*No!* No, I swear I've done exactly what I was told!"

"To the point when your conscience got the best of you and you started talking to Jonah Lund and his associate, hmm?"

Finley gave her a smug little smirk, one of disappointment. He sat on the bed beside her.

Earlier he'd considered how attractive she was, despite the

obnoxious personality. She looked even better now, on a bed, the tied wrists and ankles adding a bit of kink. She pulled in a decent revenue as one of the refined, not quite one of the top earners, but far from the worst. He wondered if being tied up wasn't so very unfamiliar to her.

"Who is he?" Finley said. "The tall guy in the dark clothes."

"I ... I don't know. I swear. I guess he's another one of Jonah's private detectives."

Finley thought about the man, everything he'd seen throughout the day. How the man had spotted Finley at the parking garage; no one had ever been able to smell Finley out before. How deadly efficiently the man had taken down two of Finley's men. Brutally fast. Mechanical. Precise.

Finley shook his head. "That guy's no private detective. He's a pro."

Kim started crying again. "Are you gonna kill me?"

"We want answers, Kim. There are always ways to get them. And, yes, those ways could end up killing you."

She wailed. "W-w-what are you going to do?"

Finley grinned at her. "Oh, not me. The big guy wants to take care of you personally."

CHAPTER THIRTY-THREE

THEY SAT in the Grand Cherokee at the edge of a gas station parking lot, near the air pump, which was still humming after a guy in an S-10 had stopped to fill his tires. A steady bustle of vehicles, people on foot zigzagging around them, sipping their freshly purchased mega-cups of soda, unwrapping candy bars. Metallic clicks of gas pumps being turned on and off. Gurgling nozzles. Impatient conversations.

When they'd gotten a safe distance from the overpass, and when it was clear they hadn't been followed, Silence had told Gavin to pull over.

Because they needed to regroup in a major way.

Silence had a children's book in his hands. *The Secret of Summerford Point*. It had a bright blue cover featuring a plucky-looking, auburn-haired girl, smiling but determined. Behind her was a coastal town bathed in nighttime darkness, spotted with streetlights.

He returned to the page in the back, the one Gavin had pointed out, a blank page that had been covered with two columns of Amber Lund's handwritten notes.

Silence had been pouring through the notes, combining his findings with the dead woman's.

And so far, nothing was making sense, nothing was telling him what had happened to Amber...

...or how he was going to find Kim Hurley.

Kim had told him she was involved in Amber's disappearance. On the surface, that would make Silence dismiss the idea of trying to find where Mr. Accord had taken her.

But Kim hadn't had the full opportunity to tell her story before she was abducted, and she had seemed incredibly remorseful, which led Silence to believe that while she may have been involved in Amber's disappearance, that didn't necessarily mean that she was involved in her death.

Silence was good at reading people. C.C. had told him this was a positive quality, something to never lose, something that would always root him in his humanity. He didn't sense evil in Kim Hurley.

Naturally, helping her wasn't part of the original mission parameters set forth by Falcon. But he was going to anyway.

She was worth saving.

If for no other reason than to help find out what had happened to Amber.

In the back seat, Jonah was clearly having similar thoughts about Kim. He said, for the second time, "It's my fault. Mine, dammit. They took Kim because of me."

Silence looked into the rearview mirror, made eye contact with him. Jonah's face was twisted, grimacing. He rolled his head on the headrest, side to side, over and over.

Silence returned his gaze to the book. And when Jonah spoke again, Silence held up a hand, quieting him. It was time for rationality, not emotion.

He pulled out his PenPal and took the mechanical pencil from the spiral binding. Typically, he could convey what he needed to others through his abbreviated speech or through non-verbal cues. But sometimes he simply needed to get a lot of info out at once, so he turned to his notebook.

He scribbled out some notes.

C11 gets prostitutes by offering women literal Get Out of Jail Free cards

The enforcers are "foremen" — also criminals they've let off the hook

Corruption starts with C11 but has influences in the rest of OPD, as well as the state police and highway patrol

The guy running the show is the Oil Man

He put the notebook on the armrest. Gavin and Jonah hunched over it, read what he'd written.

"Okay," Jonah said. "But how does this help us now?"

Gavin picked up the notebook, squinted at a detail. "One of the thugs back at the overpass said that Amber had gone there asking about the Oil Man."

Silence reached out, and Gavin handed the notebook back to him. He looked over the note he had written, scratched his chin.

He opened the children's book to the back page and the note he had in mind:

Oil Man = Warren

He put his finger below this note, pointing it out to Gavin. "Warren? Character in book?"

Gavin nodded. "Right. The town's police chief. Kara goes

to him about police involvement at the docks, but he doesn't take her seriously."

Silence leaned his head back against the headrest, gazed at the headliner.

Since Amber was using this book to guide her own investigation, there must be something to the fact that she thought the Oil Man was synonymous with the corrupt police chief.

But specifically how, Silence couldn't know without fully understanding the story.

Silence looked at Gavin, held up the book, and flipped the bookmark, which was about ten percent in from the end of the book.

"Tell story," Silence said. He swallowed. "To point where..." He swallowed. "...you left off."

Gavin looked at him for a moment, squinting, confused. Then a look of understanding.

He began. "Okay. It starts with Kara arriving at her grandmother's in coastal Maine for a two-week stay during her summer vacation..."

———

The other two had gone quiet as Silence read *The Secret of Summerford Point*.

After listening to the recap, Silence had started his reading at the point where Gavin had left off. Silence wasn't a particularly fast reader, but it was a kids' book and the print was large; he could get through it quickly enough.

What else *could* he do at this point?

After discovering how dark Summerford's weapons-smuggling operation really was, Kara's unexpected ally O'Malley had said he was going to the docks to investigate that night's shipment from Whitehead Incorporated, a front for one of the world's largest illegal arms dealers. After the obligatory argument, O'Malley begrudgingly allowed Kara to join him. They hadn't been there long when O'Malley was abducted.

Silence continued reading.

Oh my goodness!

Kara's mind kept repeating those same three words.

Oh my goodness! Oh my goodness!

O'Malley was gone.

Taken.

She just kept seeing those eyes, over and over, another repetition in her mind. O'Malley's stern face, beaten and bloodied, captured, being dragged away by the two men.

But he'd still been calm, in control, commanding. Even in his precarious situation, he'd been able to make eye contact with Kara and give her the smallest of shakes of the head.

No, his expression had said. *Don't follow.*

And she hadn't. She'd stayed right there, around the corner of the wall. Only O'Malley knew her location, not the other men in the dock.

She felt like a coward, like she should have disobeyed him even though he was an adult, even though he was a high-ranking authority.

What should she do?

There was a voice then. From the other side of the wall. A man's voice. Someone in command.

"Just put him in the back room," the man said. "We'll deal with him after the shipment's unpacked."

Kara recognized the voice!

No, it couldn't be...

Her back was squeezed against the wall, making her even more aware of her pounding heart, her shaking limbs. She didn't know if she could move. Fright had completely enveloped her.

But she had to see who belonged to that voice.

She had to confirm.

Her fingers quivered as she put both hands onto the cold, dusty concrete, pushed, and turned herself around. She reached up and grabbed the sill of the window under which she was hiding, the window that looked into the other room. She slowly pulled herself up until she could see.

There was O'Malley, being dragged to a door on the far side of the other room.

And there was the man giving the commands, the man she'd suspected.

It was Police Chief Warren.

Silence paused for a moment before he turned the page. He rubbed his eyes.

A big reveal in the story. Warren was corrupt. Summerford's police chief was the one running the weapons-smuggling operation.

But what good did knowing this do for Silence? A dark, nagging thought whispered to him from somewhere on the rational side of his brain—reading this children's book could be a waste of time, one that could cost a person her life.

Sure, Amber Lund had been following the story as she conducted her investigation, but that didn't mean she had been taking it so literally that—

And then he saw it.

As he turned the page.

Another note. In Amber's adult handwriting.

Just like Dad.

He read the first few lines of the page, which detailed a further description of Chief Warren from Kara's perspective as she hid behind the wall and peeked through the window.

Warren.

The corrupt police chief.

The one heading Summerford's illegal operation.

Silence turned to the back of the book, traced a finger down Amber's list of notes until he found the one he was looking for.

Oil Man = Warren

Then back to the page he'd just been reading.

Just like Dad.

Silence felt his face slacken.

And the other two men noticed. Jonah leaned up between the seats. Gavin squared to face him.

"What is it?" Gavin said.

Silence remembered the note he'd found in Beasley's office. Beasley, the notorious rat, had recently contacted Carlton Stokes. And someone had also contacted Beasley recently—Carlton's daughter.

Amber.

Silence fumbled for his notebook. He furiously scribbled a note and slapped it on the armrest.

Amber's father is the Oil Man. He's the one running the Well. He has Kim Hurley.

The air felt stagnant in the car after the gasping reaction of the other men.

Silence faced Gavin.

"Carlton's house." A twinge of pain in his throat. He worked up some saliva, swallowed. "You can get us there?"

Gavin nodded.

"Drive!" Silence said.

CHAPTER THIRTY-FOUR

CARLTON STOKES TOOK another sip of bourbon and savored its warm travel down his throat, into his stomach.

"Shit," he said.

He placed the tumbler on the end table beside him, next to the laptop computer, the principal component of his last-ditch effort to fix the damage.

Nothing was working out the way he had hoped. None of this was going according to plan.

For one thing, there were people in his house—the sort he didn't enjoy associating with, but the sort he needed in situations like this one. They were in his kitchen, a few feet away. Laughing. Causing a ruckus.

"Shut up!" he shouted without turning around.

They quieted.

He ran his fingers along the laptop. Things had gotten so bad he'd been reduced to *this*.

He exhaled, and it came out as much a grumble as a sigh.

It was all falling apart because of Jonah Lund. The loser, the layabout.

Jonah freaking Lund.

That was the most unbelievable part of all this. Somehow Jonah had found a man—this strange mystery man that Finley had told Carlton about—someone who had brought the light of day upon the shadowy operation, the Well, that Carlton had created so many years ago, a subcomponent of C11's already shady dealings.

And Carlton knew who the mystery man was, who he had to be.

After years in the Orlando Police Department's corrupt District C11, Carlton had heard plenty of rumors about The Shadow. Most thought he was just a legend, and for many years, Carlton assumed this to be the case. But after a while, there were too many coincidences, too many serial killers who randomly committed suicide, too many ruthless gang leaders found shot to death behind heavily guarded walls. Someone was out there. Or some*thing*. And Carlton started to believe in the myth of The Shadow.

He just never thought he would personally encounter him.

However, experience had also taught Carlton that adaptability was the most important attribute one could have, especially when one was doing things of the illegal variety.

And now Carlton would need to adapt once more.

Adaptation was how he would survive The Shadow.

He grabbed the tumbler, stopped before he raised it to his mouth. His fingertips tingled. He should quit. He needed his wits.

He put the tumbler back on the table, squeezed his fingers into fists, willing out a bit of the tingle, then grabbed the laptop and stood.

It was time to move on to the next step.

Time for adaptation.

The house was shadowy dark. He switched on a couple more lamps as he crossed the living room.

Up the stairs. His feet sank into the plush carpeting.

To the second-floor landing. Three doors—two bedrooms and a bath. One of the doors was closed.

He approached the closed door. Faint, warm light traced its edge, spilled out of the gap at the bottom.

He wrapped his fingers around the brass, lever-style door-knob, pressed down, slowly guided the door open. A slight squeal of the hinges. They would need to be oiled.

The door listed open, revealing the bed.

And the person lying on it.

Kim Hurley.

Lit by the soft glow of the bedside lamp. Her wrists and ankles zip-tied.

She screamed.

"Hello, Kim," Carlton said with a smile.

CHAPTER THIRTY-FIVE

FINLEY WAS ABOUT to jump out of his skin.

Not because of his surroundings—a modern kitchen with all the latest appliances, everything chic and shiny, an aesthetic Finley needed to adapt to if he was going to continue his upward mobility—but due to the two people with him, the only two Finley had been able to wrangle on such short notice.

Despite the sophistication and size of the Well, its decades of operation tuning it into a precision machine, there were still only so many resources, only so many would-be prisoners to whom the corrupt police had given a second chance. In a short-notice situation, the pool of hired hands could be rather shallow.

The two behind him were Hayes, a barrel-chested, light-red-haired, smiling doofus who had been apprehended for domestic violence, and Schuyler, a dope dealer wannabe hippie with long black hair, streaked with premature gray, and scraggly whiskers poking out of an acne-riddled face.

A pair of idiots. Who wouldn't shut up.

"Boss man said to keep it down," Finley said.

They quieted again.

Fortunately, Finley didn't have to look at them. He had his back turned to them as they played cards. Their game of choice was "war," a game based not on a mix of skill and chance like so many card games, but one entirely based on chance, a glorified version of high card. It was a contest fitting of these two morons.

Finley had encouraged them to play the game, and it made him feel like a babysitter to two grown-ass men. But it only took so many people to watch the monitor, a four-inch, black-and-white screen in a white plastic housing. The image on the screen was divided into equal quadrants, tiny images that Finley had to squint to study. Each was a feed from the cameras positioned around the exterior of the house belonging to Carlton Stokes, the Oil Man.

Finley reclined, stretched his back, his arms going high. He rubbed the strain from his eyes.

The chime *binged*.

He snapped back to attention, leaning forward, his face inches from the screen, so close he could feel the monitor's heat, its halo of static charge.

Excited murmuring from the dolts behind him.

"Shut up," he said without taking his eyes off the screen.

The upper left-hand image—the feed from the far end of the driveway—showed a vehicle pulling onto the property, a Jeep Grand Cherokee. The image was grainy, but as the vehicle moved to a different quadrant of the screen—the feed for the second camera, farther up the driveway—Finley could clearly see the big man, Jonah Lund's companion, in the passenger seat, his angular face, dark eyes and dark hair.

The Jeep pulled to a stop. The passenger door opened. And the big guy got out, moved toward the house with haste. Whoever was behind the steering wheel stayed back.

Finley whipped around in his seat, faced the others. "Wait

two minutes. Then go out the side door. Anyone in that Cherokee, kill them."

"What are you gonna do?" Schuyler said.

Finley turned back to the monitor. On the lower left-hand feed, he saw the big man approach the side of the house, near the porch.

A glance to the living room. Carlton was gone.

Back to the monitor. The big man drew a gun from beneath his sport jacket, a Beretta 92FS. He reached for the door handle.

Finley flashed the other two a look. "I'm gonna hang out in here."

CHAPTER THIRTY-SIX

THE DOOR WAS GLASS, framed with dark-stained wood and flanked by two sconces and a pair of sidelight windows. The house beyond was well lit.

Silence tried the doorknob. Unlocked. He threw the door open, cleared it.

And entered.

Into the bright light. Chilly air conditioning. There was the smell of fresh upholstery or maybe carpet and the sharp tang of cinnamon candles.

No people.

The house was spacious, airy, an open floor plan. Ahead was a hallway leading to the back of the house. To the side was a door, cracked open, that led to a darkened garage, evidenced by the unfinished quality of the wall beyond and the garage door opener mounted on it. Just past that door was a staircase with a dark wood banister leading to the second floor.

He glanced up to the landing. His view was partly obscured, but he could make out two doors—one open, one not. There was a bit of light coming from beneath the closed door.

His senses pulled him in that direction.

Before he could even take a step, his intuition was validated. From behind the closed door came a bloodcurdling scream.

Kim.

Silence bolted across the tiled entryway, around the sofa at the back side of the living room area, to the base of the stairs.

A sudden jolt.

Pressure on his shoulder, powerful fingers pressing into his skin and pulling him to the side, using his own rushing momentum against him, diverting his path. A gust of dry air against his skin. Darkness in front of him.

And as he stumbled through the doorway into the pitch black garage, he saw a flash of Mr. Accord.

CHAPTER THIRTY-SEVEN

CARLTON LAUGHED.

"What are you screaming about, Kim? I haven't done anything yet. I just wanted to show you."

He was on the bed, sitting a few inches from her, holding the tool in the air. An hour earlier, when Finley had called to say he'd be bringing Kim to the house, he'd stashed it in a drawer in the nightstand.

"Do you know what this is?"

Kim just stared up at the tool, shaking, sweating, tears trailing from the corners of her eyes. Carlton waited a moment, making it clear to her he would not continue until she responded. She finally shook her head.

"It's a turning tool," he said, admiring the tool himself, a long, sinuous thing, delicate and almost feminine-looking, but incredibly durable, tough. Its chiseled tip was freshly sharpened, a perfectly clean, precise edge. "Demolition has been my game since retiring from the force. But woodwork is my passion. High-end stuff. Doctors' offices. Mansions. I've built a small but enthusiastic client list. Did Amber ever tell you about any of this?"

Kim shook her head.

"You know what I like about it? The immediate feedback, the tactile sensations. You press a piece of metal, like this, to a piece of wood, and you receive an immediate response. You've changed the wood forever. Maybe for the better or maybe for the worst, but either way, you've changed it. You learn from experience, and as you improve, so do your products. Very different from police work. Or the demolition business. There are so many gray areas in those lines of work, so few opportunities for tactile feedback. But this..." He twirled the tool between his fingers. "This is real. Tactile. Receptive."

He held it closer to Kim. She cowered back into her pillow, eyes squeezing shut. The bedside lamp played off the long, thin shaft of metal coming out of a long, hourglass-shaped piece of smoothly polished ash, secured by a brass ferrule.

"It's a skew chisel, for use with a lathe. When you put a piece of sharp metal like this against a rapidly spinning piece of wood, it rounds the corners, smooths the wood to a circular shape. Leave the chisel in one spot for a while, you start changing the curves, which means you can make things like table legs, lamp bases.

"This is a fine tool. A precision piece. I don't buy crap. Hardened, tempered, high-speed steel, which holds an edge much longer than carbon steel."

He brought his free hand close to the chisel, dabbed his thumb to the upper point, the toe. Chillingly sharp.

He smiled at the chisel then looked at Kim.

"We don't *have* to use the chisel tonight, Kim."

This made her gasp. A tear fell down her cheek. Then her eyes darkened into a scowl. "How did it happen? They were just gonna scare her. Rough her up her. Didn't you tell them about her condition? *How did you let this happen?*"

Carlton smirked. Kim was in no position to be demanding answers.

He turned and reached for the laptop, which he'd placed on the nightstand, opened, and plugged into the telephone jack. He twisted it to face the bed, its rubber feet squeaking on the glass topper.

"Now, here's what you're going to do, Kim. You'll see that I've directed Netscape to the OPDCOM system. And you'll further see that the username and password fields are empty, waiting for your credentials."

He smiled at her.

"I have a message prepared and ready to go in a Word document. I'm going to copy and paste it into an email that's going to be delivered to the police from your account. The message explains you were the one who killed my daughter. You and Amber were friends, worked together at the dispatch center, and when Amber began asking too many questions and found out that you're a hooker, you panicked, thought the do-gooder was going to turn you in. So you encouraged her to take her brand-new husband to couples therapy all the way out in Titusville, getting her outside the city, in the middle of nowhere on US 50. You hired people to run her off the highway and kill her.

"But now, since Amber was such a good friend of yours, you're feeling guilty. And you want to confess. Don't worry, Kim; the Well appreciates all your, er, hard work, so we'll see that you don't fry. I don't see what other options you have. All I need from you is your username and password."

Still smiling, he placed the chisel on the glass beside the computer and poised his fingers over the keys.

Kim shook her head. Her trembling lips searched for words momentarily before she could speak. "No. I'm not going to jail for the Well. I'm going to finish what Amber started. I'm gonna bring the damn thing down."

Carlton smiled broader. "You know, Kim, I've heard you're one of our best refined ladies, but you have a tendency to be problematic. That was a very problematic answer."

He picked the chisel back up, and there was a small *cling* as its sharp tip hit the glass. He traced the chisel's toe point down her thigh, applying a bit of pressure. Her black jeans split open, curly frayed edges.

She wailed.

He put the chisel on the bedspread, stuck his fingers on both sides of the opening in the pant leg, her smooth, warm skin brushing his fingers, and tugged, splitting the tear all the way to her knee. The jeans made a satisfying sound as they ripped, and Kim screamed again.

He put his hand on her now exposed thigh, rubbed up and down. Supple, perfectly shaved, quivering at his touch. Lovely. No wonder she was so popular. He should have partaken at some point. Oh well.

He grabbed the chisel again and brought it to her skin. The edge was terribly sharp, eliminating his need for theatrics. Let the chisel do the work. He lightly, so lightly traced it along her thigh. The skin flared with goosebumps.

And then quickly, he applied a bit of pressure, pushing the toe point in with a tiny pop, piercing her flesh. A drop of blood appeared and raced down the curve of her thigh.

Kim wailed.

He continued.

CHAPTER THIRTY-EIGHT

THE DOOR SLAMMED SHUT.

Silence staggered into the darkness of the garage, his eyes glancing back to the door, to where Mr. Accord was, and saw just a thin strip of light, the glowing rectangular outline of the doorway.

The back of his leg smacked something hard, something plastic, a couple of feet tall. A mop bucket or a trashcan or a sawhorse. The sudden impact was enough to spin him around, shuffle his feet, make him reach out into the darkness for something to steady himself. He found a surface, caught his balance, something cold and hard, the side of a vehicle.

His eyes adjusted, gathering fragmental outlines of his surroundings—a workbench to his left, a utility closet by the door.

He turned, and the bit of light from the doorframe showed Mr. Accord.

Right in front of him.

What the faint light didn't show, until the very last moment, was a fist, swinging in a massive uppercut.

The blow caught Silence right under the chin, cracking

his teeth together with a sound that echoed through the garage. His head whipped back, straining his neck, future whiplash. His arms swam in circles. He staggered back again, farther into the darkness, sliding along the side of the vehicle.

Eyes forward. Mr. Accord in front of him, pulling back for a massive jab, a twinkle of confidence in his eye.

Silence reached out, wrapped his hand around the fist, stopped it before it could even move.

The look of confidence on Mr. Accord's face changed to bewilderment, a bit of fear. Silence's strength confounded lowlifes.

It wasn't the sort of strength forged with barbells and weight racks. It wasn't honed by any sort of traditional exercise program. It was a mixture of static strength, speed, explosiveness, and muscular endurance. It came from a combination of mental conditioning, isometric exercises, and repetition.

It was the sort of strength that a scumbag like Mr. Accord had never encountered.

Silence twisted the man's fist, a precise movement that brought incredible pressure on the rotator cuff. Mr. Accord bent at the waist, then looked up at him with those bewildered eyes again. With his free hand, Silence slugged Mr. Accord across the jaw. The man stumbled back.

Silence lunged for him, tightening his fist, ready for a deadly blow.

But as he stepped forward, he felt himself shift to the left, felt his surroundings shift as well, moving in a strange off-kilter manner. That first uppercut from Mr. Accord had been a doozy, but he hadn't realized that it had been devastating.

Another step. Toward Mr. Accord. Silence's hand slipped off the vehicle.

He reached under his jacket. His fingers brushed the

Beretta, fell off. Grabbed it. Pulled it from the holster. It fell from his grasp, clattered on the concrete.

Silence had had the sense knocked out of him many times in his line of work, but it always returned quickly, within minutes.

Right then, though, Silence didn't have minutes.

Only seconds.

He put his hands on his knees, straightened up, staggered to the side. Regained himself. Looked up. And in his swimming vision, he saw Mr. Accord.

Sneering.

The confidence had returned.

Mr. Accord recognized the symptoms Silence was exhibiting. He knew he'd knocked him senseless.

And so he slowly approached, sneering broader, almost gleefully, and grabbed Silence by the arm. He yanked hard and spun Silence half a revolution before releasing him.

Silence flew to the far end of the room, his shoes slapping against the concrete, deeper into darkness. Dusty, thick air. A change in direction, a twirling of his senses, and he hit something that sent a shock of pain through his back.

A set of shelves.

It cracked and collapsed upon him.

Sharp pain to his left shoulder. Something had fallen, struck him. Another blow to his head. His neck. His other shoulder. His back.

The contents of the shelves. He was being pummeled. And even in the darkness, Silence's trained senses told him what was dropping on him—metal paint cans.

He fell to his knees.

Bam! Bam! Bam!

They struck Silence all over—left, right, top, bottom. On his stomach now. Sharp edges cracked into his back, through his clothes, through his skin, into his muscle.

More cans falling. A crack to the back of the skull, hard, an instant headache.

And with a final metallic *thud*, the last can crashed onto the concrete beside him.

He was half-buried in the heavy cans. The palm of his left hand was pressed flat against the cold concrete, and two cans rolled to a stop in front of him. One was latex paint; the other was a smaller can, wood stain. Which would explain why there were so many damn cans. Carlton Stokes must've been a woodworking hobbyist.

Silence groaned. Pain warbled throughout his body—at the top of his head, through his core, into his feet. He moved his arm. The heavy cans tumbled around him, like stones tumbling down a precipitous mountain face.

His eyes were closed. He opened them again, scanned the garage, found the rectangular outline of light coming in from the house's interior.

And there was Mr. Accord, faintly silhouetted in the dim glow.

He stepped toward Silence.

And Silence's cheek fell to the concrete.

CHAPTER THIRTY-NINE

THE DARK LINE running down Kim Hurley's luscious thigh was only an inch long.

But it had been agony for her.

She was screaming to beat the band, and while Carlton wasn't the type to enjoy such things—he'd taken part in similar brutalities during his active days in C11 and never gotten quite the thrill from it that some of his associates had —he couldn't say he wasn't enjoying it either. Kim was quite the little dish, a spirited thing, the wild child among the refined girls; seeing her kick and scream and twist and moan so much was a bit of a turn-on.

But he wasn't doing this for fun. There was a purpose. And he needed to get it accomplished.

He pulled the chisel from her leg.

She panted.

"This can end, Kim." He motioned to the laptop. "Username and password. Then this will all be over."

She looked at him with wet eyes. The eyes went to the laptop. And back to him.

He felt the left corner of his mouth rise a bit in a smile.

He'd almost broken her.

Footsteps. From the other side of the house.

A sweep of panic flushed his skin. He turned dumbly to look at the door.

"Shut up," he hissed at Kim.

And he listened.

He remembered the big man that Finley had described, about his thoughts from a few minutes earlier, his assumption that the big man was the figure of legend.

The Shadow.

In his house.

Carlton was trapped!

He needed something, an advantage, a bargaining chip, a weapon.

Something.

Something more than a goddamn skew chisel.

He hadn't thought to bring a gun with him to his own guest room, but damn if he didn't wish he had one now.

But what could he do?

There was always an answer. Adaptation, remember? Adaptation was the answer to any question.

He looked around the room.

Carpet.

A dresser.

Nightstands, one with a laptop.

And there it was. On the far wall. The answer. His bit of ingenuity. Long, dark, decorative ropes hanging from either side of the designer drapes.

Maybe the chisel wasn't so feeble an object after all.

He went to the window, brought the bloody chisel to the left rope, started hacking. The razor-sharp edge instantly began fraying the silky-smooth threads of the rope.

Yes, adaptation. He would get through this.

And just when his confidence was reaching its peak...

He heard gunshots.

CHAPTER FORTY

BANG!

A horrible sound. A gunshot had struck Gavin's Grand Cherokee.

He'd thought he'd seen something, out in the trees, a pair of shadows among the shadows, two figures. That's why he'd kept the Bodyguard on his thigh, under his hand, his finger safely outside the trigger guard.

But he'd done that as a precaution. He didn't actually think there was someone out in the trees. What he had thought were two figures advancing toward him and Jonah in the Grand Cherokee had surely been his imagination.

But his initial intuition had been correct.

There *was* a pair of people out there.

And evidently they were out to kill him and Jonah.

"Get down!" Gavin screamed at Jonah in the backseat.

Gavin ducked beneath the steering wheel just as another round struck the vehicle.

BANG!

The shots had come from the left, the same side of the wooded driveway where Gavin had seen the two figures in the shadows. He scrambled to the other side of the Grand Chero-kee, over the center console, waving his hand for Jonah to follow.

Gavin threw open the passenger door.

Only to find one of the men there, a submachine gun in his hand.

Gavin didn't realize he was doing it, but his right hand raised the Bodyguard, and his finger pulsed the trigger twice, two rounds, straight into the man.

The vicious-looking gun in the man's hand went off, a blaze of fire from its barrel and more rounds thudding into the sheet metal.

Thwack! Thwack! Thwack!

A fiery explosion in Gavin's shoulder. Warm moisture dappled his cheek, his lips, the corner of his eye, squinting it shut. He tasted blood.

Pain had never been so palpable. Or so horrible. It went in waves through his body, shuddering and awful.

But a quick glimpse out the door revealed that he'd given as good as he'd gotten.

In fact, he'd given even better. The other man lay in a motionless pile at the edge of the woods.

With his good hand, Gavin clenched the passenger seat cushion and pulled himself over the seat, landed with a jolt on the concrete driveway. Jonah scrambled out as well and crouched next to him.

They bolted for the trees, Jonah putting an arm around Gavin's back, steadying him. They positioned themselves around two trunks, peered toward the mangled Grand Chero-kee, its hole-riddled sides and shattered glass, toward the other side of the driveway, where the other man still lurked.

Gavin held up a finger. And they listened.

A slight rustling in the trees on the other side of the driveway.

Gavin turned to Jonah, whose eyes were wide with fright, and mouthed, *Stay put.*

Gavin scuttled back toward the Grand Cherokee, Jonah reaching out behind him, those wide eyes begging him to halt.

Back into the vehicle, his torso over the center console, staying low, beneath the bottom edge of the window, out of sight.

The engine was still running, and he snaked below the steering wheel, pushed the brake pedal with his left hand, and with his right, pinched the button on the gear selector in the center console and pulled it down into the neutral position. He reached beneath the driver seat, fingers exploring, and found his steering wheel club. He shoved it against the gas pedal.

The engine roared.

He jammed the opposite end of the club into a contour of the floor panel.

And with one swift movement, he pulled the gear selector down, out of neutral and into drive, and jumped from the open passenger door.

The Grand Cherokee rocketed off, the passenger door whacking Gavin in the hip painfully.

He hit the concrete again, rolled, ending in the prone position, and saw the Grand Cherokee barreling away.

He also saw flashes from the tree.

Muzzle flash from an automatic, another submachine gun like the dead man had used, firing at the vehicle.

Tat-tat-tat-tat!

Gavin had three rounds left in his five-round revolver. He squeezed the trigger rapidly, emptying the rounds in the vicinity of the muzzle flash.

And the muzzle flash stopped.

There was a *thump* of something falling and the crackle of branches.

Then a loud metallic crash in the distance as the Grand Cherokee ran itself into a tree trunk.

And then quiet.

Just the sound of the Grand Cherokee's engine.

For a while, Gavin had felt nothing but adrenaline.

But now the pain returned. Flushing over him.

He collapsed onto the concrete.

CHAPTER FORTY-ONE

SILENCE WAS HURT. He was hurt badly.

But not *that* badly.

Not as badly as he was letting on.

Among the many deadly skills Silence had in his Asset toolbox, one of the deadliest wasn't at all violent.

Deception was a powerful tool. Silence could be a damn good actor when he wanted to.

So he could get past the pain of the beating he'd taken from the cans that now buried him.

And he could make the situation look a lot worse than it really was.

He groaned, loudly, as he got to his knees.

Mr. Accord approached at a slow walk, all the confidence fully returned to his smile. "You know, we've crossed paths all day, and yet we haven't said a word to each other. Haven't even made introductions. My name's Finley. And you are?"

Silence didn't respond. He just groaned again.

The groaning itself was genuine, as a fresh wave of pain rushed over his left ribs. But the volume and emphasis was all for show.

He'd made it sound as though he was on the edge.

He would continue the act.

But at the same time he kept his hand behind his back, fingers clenching a thin strip of metal, his hand weighted down.

"Not gonna give me your name? I wonder if that's because you're injured or because you just don't talk," Finley said. "See, earlier Carlton told me who he thinks you might be—a legendary vigilante, who hardly speaks, just tells his victims to 'talk.' Is that you?"

Silence didn't respond. He just grimaced, moved his right hand out of the mound of cans, making sure it was clearly visible to Finley as it shook dramatically.

And with his other hand, he tightened his grip.

"Mr. Stokes didn't want me to kill you until I figured out who you are," Finley said. "But if you're not gonna talk..." He reached to his waist, an undeniably characteristic movement, going for a gun concealed at his lower back.

It was time for Silence to drop the act.

He squeezed the paint can's handle tighter and swung up, a huge, arching path.

A full can of latex paint weighs approximately 11.3 pounds. Silence knew this from both study and experience.

A full can of latex paint can easily break a man's jaw. Silence knew this solely from experience.

This particular can wasn't entirely full, but it was close. Silence approximated its weight at a bit over ten pounds.

Which was evidently still enough weight to break a man's jaw.

Crack!

Broken bone. A moist, distorted shriek emitted from Finley's now grotesquely distorted face, mouth open, half of his lower row of teeth jutting at a bizarre angle to the rest of them. His hands went up, hovering inches from his flesh, searching without touching, confused bewilderment in his wide eyes.

Silence wouldn't let him wallow in confusion for too long.

Silence was a nice guy like that.

He swept Finley's leg, bringing him to the concrete with a loud thud.

Silence dropped, joining him on the floor, knees on either side of Finley's torso. Hands on the upper part of Finley's head, the intact part.

A swift, hard tug.

Snap.

And a clean death.

Silence stood.

His headspace was chaotic. He needed to recenter.

He took a deep breath, closed his eyes, embraced his pain, felt it surging through his body in electric waves, acknowledged it, respected it, recognized where it felt the worst, at his right trapezius where one of the first cans to fall had struck him, a tender spot on his hip, one of his toes, a deeper breath, in his center, through his core, the pain was acknowledged, another breath, his feet in contact with the floor.

Then his eyes snapped open again.

A five-second meditation.

His vision adjusted to the tiny bit of light in the garage. He spotted his Beretta, all the way against the far wall. He crossed the room, retrieved it. To the door, threw it open, cleared it. And he cautiously proceeded back into the house.

As soon as he rounded the corner, he saw Kim and Carlton Stokes at the second-floor landing. Carlton had a sharp object to her throat, some sort of tool, one so out of place that it took Silence a moment to recognize it.

It was a chisel.

Kim had a crude noose around her neck, made of decorative, shiny rope, its ends frayed and fuzzy. One end was tied to the banister.

"You're The Shadow, aren't you?" Stokes said. "The silent vigilante. The Angel of Death, come to stop me. C11 has been a way of life for a select group of people for years, *decades*, and you came in and destroyed that in one day.

"My daughter was trying to destroy it too. I never wanted kids, but my wife, God bless her soul, couldn't live without one. And then she passed away when Amber was only three, leaving me to raise the damn cripple. When Amber got all adult-like, her little wannabe detective skills kicked in, and she decided she was going to investigate C11, found out about the Well, was going to expose us. She asked me to come clean. I told her I would. After she got married—just let me see my daughter married before I face the music. So you know what I did?"

He looked intently at Silence.

"I had the bitch killed."

Silence bristled.

Kim wailed.

A deep dread in Silence's stomach. It flushed throughout the rest of his body, coursing over the pain, overtaking it.

The entire day—from the briefing Falcon had given him, to the press conference, listening to Stokes's speech at the police headquarters, to Ray Beasley's townhouse, to the shootout at the slum—Silence had known Carlton Stokes was a creep, felt it in his bones, known that somehow Amber's death was related to Carlton's involvement with C11.

But the thought that Stokes would have his own daughter murdered hadn't materialized. Not for a second.

Silence tried to visualize the moment—a man sitting down, at his desk, or maybe the kitchen table, weighing his options, making a choice, picking up a phone and ordering a hit on his daughter.

The vision was so dark that it was lost in fog, unimaginable.

And it was only then that Silence realized what a twisted adversary he was facing.

"That's right, Mr. Shadow," Stokes continued. "I wasn't going to let my daughter bring an end to the Well. And I'm not going to let you either. I'm leaving now, and you're going to stay. Because if the rumors are true, if you're as valiant as they say, I know what you'll do next."

He shoved Kim hard.

A scream.

And she fell off the balcony.

CHAPTER FORTY-TWO

SILENCE WAS ALREADY BOUNDING to the staircase before Kim's descent completed.

Her body snapped into position, twanging the crude noose tight.

But her neck didn't break.

People often associated hanging with strangulation, but another common outcome—one that was often the desired outcome, in fact—was a broken neck.

As Silence ran over to her, he glimpsed Stokes darting past, down the stairs and out the door to the garage.

The bastard was going to get away—for now—but at least Stokes would find the curly-haired present Silence had left for him splayed on the concrete floor of his garage.

Silence put his hands beneath Kim's boots, lifted, took the pressure off.

Kim gasped. Heaving breaths.

Silence gave her a moment to catch her breath then turned around, spinning to face the staircase, juggling her feet between his hands.

"Grab the railing," he said.

She did, and Silence eased his hands off her feet until she was dangling from the balusters under her own power. Her fingers screeched against the varnish.

"I can't hold on!" she screamed.

Silence bolted up the stairs, three steps at a time.

"I'm slipping!"

As he reached the halfway point, he heard cracking wood. The balusters.

To the landing. Silence dropped to the carpet, reached through the balusters, one of which had snapped. He grabbed Kim's wrist.

A glance at the knot a couple of feet above his head.

With the railing between them, with her dangling from his grip, and with a rope connecting her neck to the handrail, there was only one way to get her free.

The handrail had to come down.

Silence reared back and drove his shoulder into it. A stab of pain. And a cracking sound from the balusters.

"*What are you doing?*" Kim screamed.

Silence shifted his weight back, thrust forward again. A shock of pain from the irritated spot on his trapezius where one of the paint cans had struck him.

The whole handrail wobbled. A few feet away, a crack lightning-bolted into the sheetrock where the rail met the wall.

Kim slipped. Her sweaty palms screeched down his forearm. He had her by the fingers now.

Only by the fingers.

One more slip, and he'd lose her.

They'd been lucky once already that she hadn't broken her neck.

Silence wasn't one to test his luck.

So he gritted his teeth, pulled his torso back as far as he could, and channeled all of his energy into his shoulder.

Crack!

The railing gave.

Pieces of the handrail and balusters flew into the open air, twisted in descent, then clattered on the floor below. And with one swift motion, Silence pulled Kim onto the landing.

They sat for a moment. Gathering themselves. Pain buzzed in Silence's shoulder. His chest heaved. He was more out of breath than he'd realized.

"I know where he's going," Kim said. "Amber kept me up to date with her investigation. She found out that Carlton had a contingency plan. If there was ever a catastrophe with the Well, he was going to destroy the record room where everything about C11 is stored. It's at the Northwest Community Police Station. Some of the records are paper, but a lot of them are on servers. He'd have to..." Her eyes widened. "Blow it up!"

A connection crackled in Silence's mind. Carlton Stokes's post-police-retirement line of work. He said it out loud. "Demolition."

Kim nodded, her eyes still panic-wide. "That office is staffed all day, every day. People will die!"

"You can get us there?" Silence said.

She nodded quickly.

Silence jumped up, grabbed her forearm, and yanked her to her feet.

"Let's go," he said, already streaking down the stairs.

CHAPTER FORTY-THREE

JONAH GRUNTED as he readjusted his hold on Gavin. It was amazing how heavy a human form could be when it was completely limp. Alive. But completely limp.

Jonah wasn't the strongest of men, but he'd still assumed that moving his former uncle-in-law to the mangled Grand Cherokee would be easier than this.

Although Gavin was still breathing, his eyes were barely open, barely registering the things Jonah said to him. And he wasn't moving. At all. Dead weight.

There was so much of the man's blood on Jonah's hands it was even more difficult to get a grip.

Gavin's face had gone horribly pale. And his eyes were closing, his head rolling to the side.

"Got to keep you talking, buddy," Jonah said, as much to himself as to Gavin.

He needed to keep Gavin cogent. As physically weak as Jonah knew himself to be, he was even less skilled in medicine. But he assumed that if Gavin stopped talking, he might stop living.

Keep him talking.

He gave him a smile. "Who knew you were such a gunslinger, huh?"

No reply from Gavin.

Jonah checked.

Still breathing.

Just very, very pale.

Jonah repositioned his grip, grabbing lower, under Gavin's ribs, a better handle. The patches of Gavin's blood grew cold, sticky.

Headlights from the other end of the drive. By the house. An engine fired up, and a vehicle came down the driveway in their direction, quickly. When it was halfway down the drive, Jonah recognized the Honda Accord.

The guy who'd been following him and Brett all day.

Shit!

What could he do now?

Jonah's heart pounded as he tried desperately to pull Gavin in the opposite direction, back to where they'd come from, to some form of cover.

But his fears were quickly allayed.

Because he saw Brett driving, Kim in the passenger seat.

The car came to a stop. Brett and Kim got out, and Brett ran over and without a word grabbed Gavin from the opposite side. Gavin suddenly moved, dragged primarily by Brett. Jonah was barely helping.

As they got closer to the Grand Cherokee, the damage became more apparent. Half the windows were shattered through, and the windshield was spider-webbed. Holes riddled the sides.

"Two guys came and shot the hell out of his Jeep," Jonah said. "He took them down."

Brett glanced on either side of the driveway, saw the bodies, nodded. He grabbed the door handle on the Grand

Cherokee's passenger door, yanked. It didn't budge. He pulled harder, and the mangled door came open with a screech.

"Get to hospital," Brett said.

Jonah felt a quick wave of panic. "I don't know this area."

Kim stepped toward them. "There's one a mile from here, down the road, then north on 441."

Jonah took another look at the vehicle. It looked like shit, but the tires were intact and the engine was running. If he could get the thing in gear, he could get to the hospital.

Gavin's feet dragged on the concrete as Brett pulled him into the passenger seat and buckled him in. Gavin grunted, his first utterance for some time.

Brett ran back to the Accord, and Kim followed suit, opening the passenger door.

For a moment, Jonah hadn't been too concerned about getting to the hospital. He had Brett back, the big man who *was* strong, *was* a leader. But now it looked like he was going to lose him.

"Where are you going?" Jonah yelled out to him.

Brett looked at him. "TCB."

CHAPTER FORTY-FOUR

"THIS IS IT," Kim said. "The northwest office."

They'd been driving for fifteen minutes, Kim navigating from the passenger seat. And when she pointed out their destination, Silence was initially taken aback. It didn't look like a police station, more like a bank. One-story. Brick. Very plain, with subdued landscaping fitting of a big chain bank—little bushes and obligatory palms, red mulch.

Silence turned left at the light, pivoting around the corner of the building toward the parking lot in the back, and as he did, the similarities with a bank were even more apparent, as there was a covered drive-through area in the back. Probably *had* been a bank at one point.

"What type—" A slice of pain in his throat. He grimaced, swallowed. "Of vehicle?"

Kim gave him a confused look. "What type of car does Carlton drive?"

Silence nodded.

"I don't know."

That was going to make things a lot more challenging.

Silence rolled to the rear of the parking lot, looking into

the idle, darkened vehicles as they passed by. He pulled into an empty slot at the back row, hopped out, and took the Beretta from its shoulder holster.

As he closed the door, he looked through the windshield to Kim, swiped his hand down. Kim took his meaning and ducked below the dash, out of sight.

He traced along the vehicles in the nearest row, peeking inside. He didn't have time to check each one, so he got as good of a view as he could through each vehicle's windshield. But that didn't mean Carlton wasn't crouched below a dash as he'd instructed Kim to do.

Silence would have to take his chances.

Another row. More darkened cars. No signs of people.

And then he heard an idling engine.

Somewhere a row or two up, its sound muffled by the noise coming from the street beside him, a steady flow of evening traffic.

Another row up. Was the idling sound coming from the parking lot? Or from the street?

For a moment, he considered bolting for the building, abandoning the parking lot search, but the idea of running into a police station armed and with a broken, raspy voice blabbering in broken English about a records room and a former cop and—

An engine roared.

Tires chirped.

Beside him.

Silence had just enough time to jump, enough spring in his feet to avoid the grill, maybe the hood.

But not the windshield.

He smashed into it.

The glass shattered against his shoulder, absorbing his impact, his weight, enveloping him like a brittle, crackling blanket.

He rolled over the top of the vehicle, bounced off the trunk, and landed hard on the blacktop.

His breath was ripped from his lungs, burning the scarred inner workings of his throat.

A groan trickled from his lips.

His eyelids closed. He forced them open.

A black Lincoln sedan idled in front of him, its windshield destroyed. A confetti mess of glistening safety glass sparkled the blacktop. The driver-side door opened. A pair of shoes stepped out. The door shut. The shoes approached.

The groan on Silence's lips grew louder as he turned his head.

And saw Carlton Stokes strolling in his direction.

CHAPTER FORTY-FIVE

THE ELECTRONIC BEEPING that represented Gavin's heart rate came slow and steady from the EKG.

A mound of bandages bulged off his shoulder, and an IV was connected to his arm, dulling his world.

For a while, his senses had left him. He remembered taking down the final thug outside Carlton's house. He remembered gasping on the concrete, motionless. And then everything else had come in flashes.

Jonah racing over to him, asking if he was okay, if he could move.

Bits of conversation he couldn't remember. He'd found a bit of strength, enough to speak.

Flashes of Jonah. His feet. His hands.

Shuffling noises and pain.

Jonah had tried to get him to the vehicle.

Headlights. The crunching sound of tires. And then there was the big guy, Brett. Kim Hurley—she'd been there, too.

The two men had moved Gavin. And his eyes had closed.

He was in the Grand Cherokee.

Then a long hallway. Bright lights. The smell of cleaners, medical supplies.

Green scrubs. White jackets. Questions he didn't answer.

And then nothing. Until a few moments ago when he'd woken up to the EKG and the IV.

A sound from the other side of the room. He stole his attention away from the IV in his arm, and it took a surprisingly long time for his face to turn toward the door.

Morphine, he assumed.

Jonah entered the room, and Gavin found his eyes, nodded.

Jonah moved Gavin's satchel from the chair beside the bed and sat.

"Thank you," Gavin said and tried to smile.

"No sweat. How ya feeling?"

"Drugged-up. Aside from that, I feel like I have a hole in my shoulder." Gavin grinned and pointed to the satchel, which was now on the linoleum, leaning against the chair. "Hand me that."

Jonah complied, grabbing the bag and placing it gently at the side of the bed, within Gavin's reach. Jonah pulled back the top flap for him, then returned to the chair.

Gavin reached inside the bag, grabbed the VHS tape, handed it to Jonah. "Watch it."

Jonah looked down at the tape, which he now held in both hands. He looked back up. Began to protest.

Gavin cut him off. "Do it."

Jonah glanced down again. And then he stood. He looked at Gavin for a moment. "Thanks."

He left.

Gavin reached into the bag again and rummaged through textbooks and notepads until he found what he was looking for.

The Secret of Summerford Point.

He held the book with the same reverence that Jonah had just held the videotape.

Then he opened it.

And he read.

CHAPTER FORTY-SIX

CARLTON CLENCHED the briefcase as he slowly approached the injured man on the ground.

The briefcase had some heft to it, tugging the handle into his fingers. Two liters of the good stuff were stored inside.

Carlton had been right when he'd thought that Kim Hurley and the big man might be only minutes behind him, that somehow, between them, they would have figured out where he was going. That was why he'd waited in the parking lot for them. Just in case.

It had been a good gamble.

Although he'd left what had seemed like an impossible situation behind at the house—Kim hanging from a home-made noose, which had been tied securely both to her neck and to the handrail—Carlton also had strong suspicions that the big man was The Shadow. And the only thing that would confirm those suspicions would be if the man had freed her and chased him down within minutes.

Which he had.

The man lying before him in the parking lot was The Shadow.

But since Carlton had taken the extra precaution, taken the gamble, waited for them, just in case, The Shadow was now incapacitated.

The man's pistol was several inches away from his outstretched hand, and as the man's pained eyes looked up to find Carlton, his fingers dumbly reached for it.

Carlton stepped up beside him, put his toe against the gun, casually brushed it away, then looked down upon the man. "Shadow Man, you've ruined a way of life that good people spent decades building. Years of hard work, scratching and crawling, destroyed in one night!"

He kicked the man hard in the ribs.

The man yelled out in pain, and when he did, the voice was raspy and horrible, almost mechanical yet also earthy, the sort of sound that Carlton was used to hearing from his demolition equipment.

Just the type of voice that The Shadow was rumored to have—deep and growly, unnatural.

Further confirmation.

"You destroyed something that's taken care of families."

He gave another kick.

"Loved ones."

Another kick.

"Medical bills, college tuitions."

Another kick.

The Shadow writhed in agony.

"And you come in here on some sort of self-righteous vendetta, just like my little bitch of a crippled daughter. Well, you may have ruined things, but you won't ruin me. I'm in the demolition business, sir. Typically, we work with manual construction demolition—excavators, wrecking balls, things like that. But more and more, I've been getting into bigger projects that require implosion. You know, controlled demolition. That gives me access to some really interesting materials."

He held up the briefcase.

"Even a small amount of nitroglycerin can make one hell of a boom. And I only need a little. Just enough to destroy the record room in that building." He pointed behind him. "We've done a good job covering our tracks, but there are certain government records we just can't alter. Only an act of God or, say, some sort of explosion will wipe those records." He reached into his pocket, removed the remote detonator, and gave it a little shake. "Drop off the briefcase, go back to my car, push this button, then all your heroics here will have been for nothing."

He kicked The Shadow again. Harder.

He lined up for another kick...

And felt a jolt of agonizing pain. From his back.

He screamed.

Then lurched forward, looked behind him.

A knife stuck out of his shoulder, wooden handle, its blade half buried.

No. Not a knife.

A skew chisel.

His skew chisel.

Kim Hurley was behind him. She tried to pull the tool from his back. Another rush of pain. The chisel held.

Carlton backhanded her, and she spun around, flopping onto the blacktop a few feet away from The Shadow.

Carlton grimaced as he grabbed the handle. And he screamed again as he yanked the chisel from his shoulder.

Blood streaked off its tip, dripping onto the ground.

He looked down at Kim. Conscious. Barely.

He scoffed and tossed the tool into the darkness of the parking lot. It clattered somewhere in the distance.

Another look at the two piles of waste before him, then he felt the reassuring weight of the briefcase.

It would all be over in a few minutes.

He turned and headed for the building.

CHAPTER FORTY-SEVEN

THE APARTMENT LOOKED menacing as Jonah unlocked the door and swung it open. Dark. Eerie. Full of specters.

And it wasn't just the visuals—none of the lights were on, the only illumination coming in through the closed blinds and the little lights on the stove and the microwave—but the *feel* of the place.

Something about the sensation was familiar to Jonah, and it took him only a moment to recognize what it was. The feeling of returning to a deceased person's living space. He'd experienced it only once before, three years ago when his grandfather passed. Stepping into the house for the first time after, to help his grandmother move some of her boxed items, there had been a strange feeling of the grotesque to the place. His grandfather had lived there. And, in the bed in the back, he had died. The halls, the doorways, the recliner in the living room, the dining room table all carried his image. There was the feeling of emptiness, the chill of an autumn day with an incongruously sunny sky.

And now Jonah's very own apartment had this feeling. Amber had lived here for two wonderful weeks.

She'd been his wife.

He found himself moving toward the television, the door closing behind him. The tape went into the VCR. A few mechanical whirs from inside the machine as it accepted the tape.

Jonah dropped onto the sofa, not bothering to turn on a light. He grabbed the two remote controls from the coffee table. Elbows on his knees. He pressed a button. The TV flashed on. Another button on the second remote. The VCR came alive, more whirs from its insides.

Jonah looked at the remote in his hand. His thumb hovered over the PLAY button.

And hovered.

And hovered...

He sucked his lower lip between his teeth. Bit down. Released.

Pressed the button.

Cloth, filling the screen. A T-shirt. Light green. Green was her favorite color. The VCR displayed *PLAY* in the upper left-hand corner, an empty timecode field in the right. The blurry green cloth shuffled in front of the lens as she fidgeted with the video camera.

She stepped away. The camera auto-focused, bringing the back of the shirt into clarity, blonde hair, the curves of a feminine figure stepping away toward a metal folding chair, limping slightly, left foot shuffling on the floor.

She sat.

Faced the camera.

And smiled.

Amber.

Jonah gasped.

"Shit!"

He pressed PAUSE on the remote, threw it onto the

cushion beside him, looked away from the screen, to the ceiling, his eyes welling.

He couldn't do this.

He couldn't watch it.

CHAPTER FORTY-EIGHT

SILENCE STRUGGLED TO SEE, to think. His usual chaotic brain space was further muddled by the beating he'd just received.

But the flashes of recent memory, the bits and pieces of Carlton Stokes's words, told him that Stokes was on his way to complete his task.

Nitroglycerin in a briefcase.

Destroy the records and maybe some innocent lives, too.

Get off scot-free.

It was a macabre bit of clairvoyance.

But the future was always changeable. With enough will.

Silence's eyes wanted to stay shut, but he forced them open and looked toward the building.

Stokes was about a quarter of the way across the parking lot.

Silence brought his hand to his jacket, to his shoulder holster. Empty.

That's right. He'd lost the Beretta.

He glanced to the side.

There it was. A couple of feet away.

Carlton was another row farther into the parking lot, another row closer to the building.

Silence moved his hips toward the gun, put a little pressure to the ground, grimaced, and dragged his torso closer, his shoulder scraping the concrete.

His fingers touched metal.

Carlton was halfway through the parking lot.

Silence got his fingers around the Beretta. Lifted it. Heavy. It shook in his hand.

With another surge of reserve strength and a groan that sent pain roiling through his throat, he rolled onto his stomach.

He lined the sights on Stokes's back. A difficult shot. But he had it.

He would need to fire several rounds. Doing so could send several errant bullets at the building.

And there was no guarantee the rounds would bring Stokes down. If he was hit but managed to stay on his feet, he could change his trajectory, get out of Silence's line of sight, and slip into the building.

With the nitroglycerin.

Better idea.

Silence pulled the Beretta slightly down and to the left.

The sights landed on the briefcase.

One well-placed round was all it would take.

Stokes was closer now, only a couple of rows away from the building.

A scuffling sound from the concrete beside him. Getting closer. Kim had recovered and crawled to him.

"Are you ... Are you doing what I think you're doing?"

Silence closed his eyes. Took a deep breath. Felt the breath at his core, the center of his being, sensed the cool, humid air on his cheeks, the bit of heat and disruption inches beside his arm that was Kim, felt his touch points, where his body was touching the earth, bumpy blacktop poking through his pants, his jacket, placing pressure on his thighs, elbows, and forearms.

A two-second meditation.

He opened his eyes.

And now his hands were still, the sights aligned steadily on the briefcase.

He squeezed the trigger.

BAM!

A blinding flash. A twenty-foot fireball.

A fraction of a second later, a wave of power and heat rushed over him.

Kim yelled out, put her hand on his back.

The heat passed. Silence's eyes had closed again, not in meditation this time but from instinctive protection.

He opened them. And saw, through the flames, people running out of the building, gawking at the fire. Screams, yelling.

Stokes had been correct. A small amount of nitroglycerin *did* make one hell of a boom.

"Come on!" Kim screamed.

Silence tried to stand. Couldn't. Kim hooked him beneath the armpits, helped him off the ground. He threw an arm over her shoulder.

She hobble-walked him, as quickly as they could, to the back of the parking lot, to the Accord. She opened the passenger door, shoved him in.

And a moment later she was behind the wheel. She fired up the engine, threw the gear selector into drive, and peeled around the closest exit, onto the street.

CHAPTER FORTY-NINE

As GAVIN TURNED THE PAGE, his heart sank.

He'd reached the final few paragraphs. A single, centered, three-letter word looked at him from halfway down the page.

END

The end of the book.

He didn't want it to end.

Reading *The Secret of Summerford Point* had somehow reconnected him to Amber. Not only had it shown him how she had conducted her investigation into CII, but it had also projected him back to the younger years, a blanketed Amber curled up against his side on the orange couch in Carlton's old house, warm against his arm, her smooth hair brushing his neck as she rested her cheek on his shoulder, the occasional questions.

How would Kara know he was going to be there?

What does "ascertain" mean?

Do you think O'Malley will make it?

He sighed.

The story had steamrolled to an exciting end. With O'Malley captured and with the new understanding that Police Chief Warren was the one behind the evildoings in Summerford, Kara had struggled to find her courage.

She had a choice before her: summon her bravery, disobey an adult's command, take a risk; or play it safe, follow the rules, and leave her new friend to his peril.

For a while, fearful paralysis ensnared Kara, her decision-making teetering between action and inaction, tossed about by opposing gusts of uncertainty and hesitant resolve.

Then she remembered what Grandmother had told her after they left the play the night before: *And what did we learn from that story, Kara? A lady must make a noble decision even when there are more convenient options.*

Grandmother's words emboldened her. She searched the marina outside the port until she found a rowboat among all the sailboats, yachts, and fishing boats. Kara didn't know how to operate a motor, let alone any of the other components of a powered boat, but Father had taught her how to row, and she was darn good at it, much stronger than she looked, Father had told her.

She stealthily rowed the boat back to the port, approaching from the quiet side, unnoticed by O'Malley and his men, who were still unloading the crates from Whitehead Incorporated. With some experimentation, she figured out how to use O'Malley's fancy camera and used it to take a series of photos that, when developed, would reveal weapons being pulled out of Whitehead crates with Summerford officers and Chief Warren supervising.

After taking the photos, she slipped into the building, found O'Malley, created a diversion to distract the men guarding him, and in the few brief moments of relative safety, she untied him from the chair to which he was bound. While he was disappointed in her for disobeying him, he was also very grateful.

And impressed.

The next morning, Kara was back at Carlito's Café with Grandmother. But it wasn't just the two of them this time. O'Malley was there too—cleaned up, fake scar removed from his face, and being very gentlemanly to Grandmother. On the black wrought-iron table was the copy of the *Summerford Herald* newspaper they'd all been reading together a few moments earlier. The shocking top headline read, *Anonymous Photos Lead to Arrest of Police Chief and Six Officers*.

They'd finished their pastries, and their coffee mugs were running low. Brunch had almost reached an end.

And for Gavin, there were only a few paragraphs left in the book.

O'Malley took another sip from his mug, peeked inside and gave an almost disappointed look before putting it on the table next to the empty saucer that had held his cruller. He put his arms behind his head and looked out over the street, smiling his casual, effortless grin, the sun playing off the edges of his dark sunglasses.

"Cute town. Real cute. I'll have to come back again someday." He turned to Grandmother. "I want you to know that the Bureau would never have been able to crack this case without your granddaughter. You have quite the little sleuth on your hands."

They both turned to Kara then. Her cheeks warmed. She glanced down, twisting her cloth napkin between her hands.

"Don't be bashful, darling," Grandmother said.

It wasn't bashfulness, necessarily, that made Kara look away. She simply didn't enjoy being in the limelight, even if only two sets of eyes powered that light. She didn't do her detective work for recognition; she did it because it was the right thing to do.

O'Malley crossed his forearms on the table and leaned closer to her. "Kara, I want to ask you: what made you decide to keep going with your investigation? There were so many opportunities for you to give up, so many dangerous situations. What kept you moving forward?"

Kara untwisted the napkin, flattened it over her lap, and pressed the wrinkles away as she considered what he'd asked.

She looked up and smiled. "I'm a detective. What choice did I have?"

O'Malley and Grandmother laughed.

Kara laughed too.

The sun was pleasant. The air tasted of the sea. Her belly was full of fine food. And she was surrounded by friendly faces and warm laughter.

Yes, this was a wonderful visit to Summerford.

END

Gavin closed the little book.

And with one hand, he brought it to his face, rubbed the edge over his cheek, whiskers scratching on the surface.

The EKG beeped.

The Secret of Summerford Point had been one of many *Kara, Kid Detective* books he'd read to Amber, and while this fresh reading had shown him a storyline not so very different from the rest of the series, the book had clearly stuck in Amber's mind all these years, so much so that she remembered it when she conducted her investigation.

He couldn't recall much about the time he'd spent reading this particular title to young Amber, but a memory had arisen moments earlier when he'd read the last words: he remembered when they'd *finished* the story, leaving Kara, Grand-mother, and O'Malley at the café and shutting the little paperback. Amber had asked him if he'd take her to Summer-ford. He'd told her it wasn't an actual place; it was fictitious. She'd contended that there were surely real-life Maine towns similar to Summerford. This had made him smile, and he'd agreed that, yes, there surely were. She'd asked if he'd take her to one of these towns. Maybe some day, he'd told her. Maybe some day.

He brought the book to his chest. Pressed it tight. Closed his eyes and tried not to cry.

He said her name.

"Amber."

And he smiled.

CHAPTER FIFTY

JONAH CONTINUED to stare up at the ceiling, its popcorn texture faintly illuminated by orange-ish streetlight sifting in through the closed blinds.

There was one other source of lighting in the otherwise darkened apartment.

The television. A few feet away from him. The light it cast onto his right cheek, his right eye—as he kept his face turned away from it—came from the image he knew it was bearing.

Amber. Sitting on the folding chair. Green T-shirt with white lettering that read, *Big Brothers Big Sisters of Central Florida*. Smiling. A fake houseplant and a wrinkly, black cloth backdrop behind her—Dr. Nogulich's permanent setup for her video do-over vows, set up in the back corner of a tiny room in her office-house.

Jonah was a coward.

That's how he'd screwed things up so much with Amber; that's how he'd been able to do the awful thing he'd done.

And now he couldn't even watch her tape.

He couldn't even look at the frozen image of her on the screen.

No...

No, he *could* do that much. He could at least look at her.

He took a breath, lowered his chin, and looked at the screen.

There she was. That smile, pure and beaming, a face that was virtuous, kind, had a tendency to giggle, which usually brought a hand to her mouth, some form of unneeded bashfulness, a playful face, a sexy face.

He picked up the remote.

And before he could stop himself, he pressed PLAY.

"Hey, Jonah," Amber said.

Jonah shuddered. He breathed out, twice, hard and rapidly.

Amber brushed a strand of hair behind her ear. "I feel a little silly talking to a camera." She stopped, looked to her right where one of the fake leaves was brushing her arm, giggled, hand to her mouth, scooted the chair away. "Everything I said in our first vows, I still mean it. So let's cut to brass tacks. You messed up, babe. And ... and I don't know if I can ever truly forgive it. People say they forgive all the time, and it's wonderful, but how often do they *really*, one hundred percent mean it? I don't know if it's possible with something like this.

"But I tell you this: maybe it's not one hundred percent, but I *do* forgive you." She paused. "Ninety-five percent, let's say." A smile. "And for something like this, I don't even think forgiveness is the most important thing. Trust is. And I give that to you, one hundred percent. I trust you, Jonah. I trust that you'll never do anything like that again, and I trust that you completely regret it. You've shown what you're made of this weekend with Dr. Nogulich. You're a good man. And I love you so, so much. Now and always."

Another smile. And she stood. Her green shirt enveloped the screen again, going blurry. Shuffling noises. A flash of static. And the screen went blue.

Jonah leaned back in the sofa, resting his head on the top of the pillow, facing the ceiling, eyes closed, and a noise came out of him. Something like joyous laughter, something like the confusing rush of overwhelming relief.

Tears dripped off the edge of his jaw.

CHAPTER FIFTY-ONE

THE ACCORD ROLLED TO A STOP. Silence unbuckled his seatbelt, ready to hop out and switch places, but after Kim put the gear selector in park, she placed both hands on top of the steering wheel and exhaled, looking out at the apartment complex.

It was quite the contrast to the one Silence had visited earlier in the day, Jonah's illustrious—if not corporately bland —setup. This one was a trio of brick buildings—two stories with additional windows along the ground revealing a third layer of semi-basement units—that were arranged in an L-shape around a grassy courtyard area with pine trees in the corners

A slight rain flecked the windshield. Kim had set the wiper speed too high, and they gave a slight screech with each pass. She didn't seem to notice, just stared out at the closed-down pool area in the center of the courtyard, encircled with yellow caution tape and a procession of sagos in sparse marble chips, a trio of sad-looking fan palms at the far corner.

Silence sensed that she was going to say something. Something deep and profound to close out their brief association. He braced himself.

But all she said was, "Damn rain."

Silence nodded.

"It'll pass in a couple of minutes. Florida weather, man!" A small, almost forced laugh. She turned her attention away from the windshield and faced him. "You really don't say much, do you?"

He shook his head.

"Your voice—may I ask? Is it, like, laryngitis or something?"

Silence looked at her. Then he exited the Accord.

He walked around the hood to the driver side where Kim stepped out, shut her door, closed the distance between them.

They stood for a moment in the pestering but unsubstantial rain, looking at the apartment complex—Kim with her arms wrapped around her chest, Silence with his hands in his pockets, the sides of his jacket tucked behind his forearms.

"What should I do?" Kim said finally.

A simple question, but her tone had been severe, heavy. It was the profundity Silence had been expecting.

He raised an eyebrow.

"I mean, you said that your organization will tie up all the loose ends, clear things up in the computers. And I'm appreciative, don't get me wrong. But ... what do I do with myself now? I didn't know they were gonna kill Amber. You have to believe me about that. But I knew they were gonna rough her up bad. I knew. *Shit!* And with her palsy. Oh god. I keep thinking about how scared she must have been. She was so sweet. She—"

Kim stopped suddenly, wiped the accruing rain from her forehead, traced the hand along her temple to her cheeks, where the rain was mixed with tears.

"You know, the highway where it happened, US 50, there's a place called Christmas. Not too far outside Orlando. Kitschy little highway town. It's got a two-hundred-foot-long building shaped like a gator. 'The World's Largest Alligator.'" She chuckled. "Amber and I went there every December, a ritual of ours. We had to go to Christmas every Christmas. She loved little pieces of Americana like that. She loved sangria too." A smile. "She wasn't much of a drinker, but she could put the sangria away. She liked it sweet. The sweeter the better."

Another abrupt stop.

"I'm rambling. I guess what I'm trying to ask you is how do I proceed? How do I continue with life knowing I got my best friend killed?"

As with earlier, when Jonah had asked Silence for advice on whether he should watch the videotape of Amber's do-over vows, Silence had no advice.

Kim Hurley's path forward was entirely determined by her own choices, no one else's.

And, as she has just stated, she'd gotten her best friend killed. Silence wasn't feeling exceedingly sympathetic.

He stepped past her, opened the driver-side door, one foot in, a hand on the wet roof, ducking inside.

"Wait!" Kim said.

He put a hand on the top of the door, fingers gripping the rubber weatherstripping, and straightened back up to his full height.

She stepped to the door, looked up at him, eyes desperate. "Please! Whatever you are, whoever you work for, you've surely seen situations like this before, haven't you?"

Silence's former life.

His *best friend.*

Lying in a puddle of blood. Her face destroyed.

A crimson-and-black crater in the back of her head, circled by dark, wavy hair.

Kim's lower lip trembled. She shook her head. Slowly. Eyes not leaving his, not blinking. Droplets of rain on her face. "How do I move forward?"

Silence took a deep breath. "Carefully."

He got in, shut the door, put the gear selector into drive, and took off.

CHAPTER FIFTY-TWO

THE FOLLOWING NIGHT.

A rumbling ball of warmth sat on Silence's lap, staring up at him with a look of sheer admiration from the inside of what looked like a tiny lampshade.

Baxter's purring felt soothing against Silence's legs. The heat was particularly evident from the cat's stomach, as it was devoid of fur. The veterinarian had indeed "shaved his belly," as Mrs. Enfield had predicted, leaving just velvety soft, strangely pinkish cat skin with wee cat nipples and a strip of white gauze covering his stitches. He wore a clear plastic cone collar—also known as an "Elizabethan collar" or a "cone of shame"—which kept him from disrupting his fresh wound, but it hadn't dissuaded his drooling, which continued to collect on the sloped plastic. Periodically, when the puddle grew large enough, gravity took over, at which point the puddle traced down the slope of the cone, off the edge, and onto Silence's pants, a new favorite pair—five-pocket, medium-dark gray, casual, slightly distressed, dress-'em-up-dress-'em-down, cotton-poly blend, now with an oblong patch of cat saliva.

Drat.

Some things never change, not even with the introduction of a cone of shame.

He sat on one of the rocking chairs on Mrs. Enfield's porch. She was in the porch swing a few feet to his right. They had been quiet for a while, watching the gentle evening unfold in front of them—a few neighbors out for nighttime walks with their dogs, a kid on a bicycle, the occasional vehicle. The sounds were faint and subtle and few in number, just a bit of noise carrying over from downtown, cars on distant streets, and Baxter's enthusiastic purring.

Silence looked down at the cat.

Baxter's eyes were slitted with contentment, and they looked right back up at Silence. When their gazes met, Baxter's purring spiked. Silence ran a hand along his back, Baxter's soft fur soothing against the coarse skin of his palms, the calluses at the base of his fingers.

Baxter was unaffected by the cone and the stitches and the discomfort in his stomach. Nothing fazed this cat.

Silence thought back to the screeching monster under Mrs. Enfield's guest bed with whom he'd fought an epic battle, trying to get the beast into a pet carrier.

Almost nothing fazed Baxter. Nothing except going to the veterinarian. And a few other select things—lawnmowers, people with a negative aura, robust squirrels.

Mrs. Enfield broke the quiet. "Sit with me, Si."

He gingerly put his hands beneath Baxter—a blip in his purring as he was lifted—and sat beside Mrs. Enfield on the porch swing. Her ghostly eyes stared across the street, into the warm glow of the streetlights.

"Let me see your face," she said.

Silence leaned over. Baxter's adoring eyes followed him.

Mrs. Enfield brought her hands up, slightly off target at

first, then found his cheeks. Her tiny, wrinkly, dry palms explored, pressing gently here and there.

"You're softened, boy," she said. "Did this business trip see you doing some fighting?"

"Yes, ma'am."

Mrs. Enfield didn't know what exactly Silence did for a living, but she was quite intuitive, and shortly after they met, she'd determined that he was involved in something violent. Like Silence, she was a good judge of character, so she'd never assumed that Silence did anything immoral. But despite her kindly-grandmother appearance and demeanor, she was also no idiot—she knew it was in her best interest to be unaware of what Silence actually did. So she never asked.

Not that Silence would have given her an honest answer. Naturally, he wasn't permitted to do so. But he was glad that she proceeded through the years in this wink-wink, I-don't-want-to-know fashion. He didn't want to lie to her, and he'd never had to.

"You were safe, though?"

"Yes."

"And you didn't drink?"

"No, ma'am."

"Good." She patted him on the knee. "Lola was upset that she didn't get to say goodbye to you."

She had told him earlier in the day that Lola had left for Tennessee only hours before he returned.

"She thinks you're a good guy, a quality man."

"I know."

More of Mrs. Enfield's wink-wink, nudge-nudge subtleties. In the same way that she never outright asked about his way of life, she'd never outright discussed Lola's subtle advances toward Silence. She knew Silence was committed to C.C. beyond "till death do you part."

Baxter finally broke his gaze off of Silence. He wanted

his momma. He rose to his feet—four tiny points of pressure on Silence's thighs—and a little squeak of discomfort sounded through his purring. Silence helped him over to Mrs. Enfield's lap, and he curled into a ball on her floral print dress, the cone propping his head up at an angle that surely was uncomfortable but, again, didn't seem to bother him.

The patch of drool on Silence's thigh began to cool almost immediately.

Gross.

"She'll be back sometime soon, undoubtedly," Mrs. Enfield said. "I'm sure she'll still think you're something special."

More of the wink-wink. *You'll have another chance with Lola*, Mrs. Enfield had said but didn't say.

"There are always new opportunities," she said. "We craft our lives moment to moment by the choices we make."

"Too true."

Silence made the choice to cherish C.C. as his perpetual fiancée. He'd made the choices that led him to become an assassin for the Watchers, which had led him here to a quiet street in the quiet neighborhood of East Hill, which had led him to a blind old woman and her cat who loved him and drooled on his leg.

This was his life now. They were his family—the old woman and her cat. It wasn't the life he wanted, nor the one he deserved. He should have been in a warm house with C.C. and at least one child, maybe a dog. There would be two vehicles. There would be discussions of preschool and PTA meetings. There would be savings accounts and investments and college funds.

And C.C.

Most of all there would be C.C.

That's not the life he was living, however. Choice determined most things, but not all. Brutal fate had intervened, a savage coup that had overcome choice for a short while.

But given he couldn't overcome this fate, he wouldn't have wanted his post-disaster life to have turned out any differently than it had.

Doling out justice, using the hideous, cruel skills he'd forged in the face of unfathomable fate, doing so honorably, salvaging his future and his soul.

And then enjoying the moments of peace that life was gracious enough to afford him. Quiet nights like this. On this porch. With his family. The old woman. The drooling cat.

Yes, Silence was content with the life he'd created through his choices.

His pager beeped.

He took it from his pocket, checked the screen.

It was Falcon.

Back to work.

ALSO BY ERIK CARTER

Silence Jones Action Thrillers Series

Novels

The Suppressor

Hush Hush

Tight-Lipped

Before the Storm

Dead Air

Speechless

Quiet as the Grave

Don't Speak

A Strangled Cry

Muted

Novella

Deadly Silence

Dale Conley Action Thrillers Series

Novels

Stone Groove

Dream On

The Lowdown

Get Real

Talkin' Jive

Be Still

Jump Back

The Skinny

No Fake

Novella

Get Down

ACKNOWLEDGMENTS

For their involvement with *Hush Hush*, I would like to give a sincere thank you to:

My ARC readers, for providing reviews and catching typos. Thanks!

April Snellings, for copy editing and editorial polish throughout.

Aunt Amy, for medical expertise.

Made in the USA
Monee, IL
22 August 2023

41452640R00138